Joy in the Morning

Joy in the Morning

Book Six
of the Enduring Faith Series

SUSAN C. FELDHAKE

ZondervanPublishingHouse
Grand Rapids, Michigan

A Division of HarperCollins*Publishers*

Joy in the Morning
Copyright © 1994 Susan C. Feldhake

Requests for information should be addressed to:
Zondervan Publishing House
Grand Rapids, MI   49530

Library of Congress Cataloging-in-Publication Data

Feldhake, Susan C.
    Joy in the morning / Susan Feldhake
        p. cm. —(Enduring faith series : bk. 6)
    ISBN 0-310-47941-X
    1. Frontier and pioneer life—Minnesota—Fiction.   2. Brothers and
sisters—Minnesota—Fiction.   I. Title.   II. Series: Feldhake, Susan C.
Enduring faith series : bk. 6.
                                                                94-29792
    813'.54—dc20   CIP

Cover design by Jody Langley
Cover art by Bob Sabin

Printed in the United States of America

    95 96 97 98 99 00 / ❖ DH / 10 9 8 7 6 5 4 3 2

For Norsky and Kraut,
treasured friends, well-loved accomplices,
and fellow members in the secret S.O.W. Association

chapter
1

Williams, Minnesota
Summer 1909

A MOURNFUL HOWL cleaved the air as the engineer hauled on the cord, signaling that the outbound Canadian National was ready to depart for points west. Slowly the train lurched ahead and the locomotive began to chug faster and faster, gobbling up miles of railbed cut through the countryside.

The steel ribbon of track running over the flat plains and winding through the bottom of ditch-like ravines had been laid in recent years by contract workers who had signed legal agreements with the railroad for this route through the thinly populated northland.

Harmony Childers gave a graceful flounce on the plush cushion as she adjusted her long skirts around her and fluffed her hair away from her face. She fanned at the sultry summer air blowing soot through the open window and swatted at a tenacious mosquito that had gained entry to the lone passenger car in this trainload of freight cars.

"I really do appreciate your taking a day off from your work at the lumber company to see me safely to Warroad, Lester," said Harmony to her brother. Then she settled back for the ride to the bustling village twenty miles from Williams, the Minnesota lumber town both the former Illinoisians now called home.

"Well, I couldn't rest easy, Sis, knowin' you were travelin' all alone," he acknowledged. "Besides, seems we don't have as much time together as I thought we would when we decided to stay here after Luke and Molly got hitched."

"I know," Harmony agreed. "You're kept busy at the lumber company, and heaven knows there's always something to do around the hospital. But I love it."

Lester gave his sister an appraising glance from the top of her bonneted blond head to the tips of her stylish black boots. He'd never seen her looking so well. "I can tell that bein' a nurse to Doc Wellingham agrees with you, all right."

She sighed. "Yes, I couldn't be happier . . . well, maybe a little happier." Harmony's tone grew wistful. "If Mama and Brad would move up here, everything would be just perfect."

"I like that idea myself, Sis. But Ma's got her roots planted so deep in central Illinois that I wouldn't be surprised if they didn't come out on the other side of the world."

"Hmmm . . . you never know."

"Yeah, she always did claim to have an itchy travelin' foot. . . ."

The two were silent as they contemplated the passing scene through the window of the coach.

"Well," Harmony said at last, "when she and Brad come back to see us—whenever that might be—they'll find Williams has changed in these last six months."

"Seems amazin' what all's happened in such a short time, doesn't it, Sis? One day at a time it doesn't seem so spectacular. But when a fellow looks back over the year, there's been a heap accomplished in a few months."

That very spring, one of the first orders of business had been the construction of a home for Dr. Marcus and Marissa Wheeler Wellingham, recently moved to the area from Chicago, along with a spacious infirmary to house sick folks.

The large, two-story, clapboard building, with a wide veranda skirting the front, had gone up in record time, for the entire community had pitched in to show their gratitude in having a resident physician of their own.

Lester smiled to himself. Wasn't it just like his kid sister to insist on calling the one-room infirmary built onto the house a "hospital"? No doubt, she already had visions of grander things for the town that was fast coming into its own.

"Isn't this land just beautiful?" Harmony asked, glancing out the window at the thick pine forests surrounding them on either side of the narrow railway.

Lester's eyes followed hers. Tall pine trees towered above the lonely landscape. Here and there, blueberry bushes, heavy with ripe fruit, hugged the ground, while lush prairie grasses undulated in the breeze of the passing train like waves in the ocean. And beyond, he knew, forest and pond alike teemed with wildlife—fish and geese and ducks and loons.

"It's beautiful, all right, in a wild kinda way," Lester agreed. "Keep a sharp eye peeled, Harmony, and like as not you'll spot herds of deer, moose, maybe even a black bear and her cubs, if you're lucky."

"Lucky?" Harmony gave a helpless shiver. "I prefer seeing wild beasts from the safety of the coach," she declared. "Why, I'd die of fright if I ever came face-to-face with a bear!"

Lester nodded. "Stay to the well-traveled paths," he cautioned reassuringly, "and there'll be enough human scent lingering to make critters give you a wide berth. And iffen you happen upon a bear and her cubs, turn tail and hurry back the way you came. Generally, though, brown and black bears are peaceable enough animals unless they feel their young'uns are threatened."

"Sounds like Mama." Harmony couldn't repress a little smile.

Lester's lips parted in a grin, revealing even white teeth. Their ma was as gentle and kindly a woman as ever lived except when she believed her children were in danger or were being treated unfairly. Then Lizzie Mathews was a force to be reckoned with.

The two fell silent, and Lester sensed that both of them were feeling the stirrings of homesickness as their thoughts were drawn to the area where they'd been born and raised. In fact, neither of them had ever really considered leaving the Salt Creek community until they'd traveled to northern Minnesota last winter for Molly Wheeler's marriage to Luke Masterson. And here, under the spell of the wilderness, they had decided to stay, knowing their skills and services were needed.

"We've got lumber camps dotted hither and yon in these great woods," Lester said, intent on redirecting their thoughts to less nostalgic paths. "I'll point them out to you as we pass by."

Harmony stared out the window. For mile after mile the surrounding stands of timber seemed indistinguishable, one from another, except when they passed through the small towns of Roosevelt and Swift. "How do you ever find your way through the woods, Les, when there are no trails?"

Lester shrugged. "Instinct, I guess, and a natural love of the land that gives me a sixth sense so I almost always know where I am. Something like a mama who can somehow pick out her own child's cry in a crowd of young'uns."

Harmony looked at him in surprise. Her handsome brother, only a boy it seemed a few short months ago, had recently taken on a new air of authority, and when he spoke of the work he knew so well, he fairly took her breath away. "I over-heard one of the lumberjacks say to Mr. Lundsten at the mercantile, Les, that you make your way through the woods like a Chippewa warrior."

Lester narrowed his eyes in speculation, then gazed at the trees flashing by for a moment before he answered. "Reckon maybe I do," he admitted. "From what I've heard, Indians respect the land same as me . . . and Pa . . . and Brad . . . and Jeremiah and Alton before them. Maybe it's just knowin' that we're only tenants, workin' the land the Good Lord made and owns."

Harmony regarded her brother with fresh appreciation. "Why, Lester Childers, I do think you've missed your calling. If I didn't know you were already making a name for yourself as a lumberman, big brother, I'd declare you should be a man of the cloth, speaking fine words from the pulpit each Sunday."

Lester gave his sister a fond smile. "I'll leave that to Reverend Edgerton, and trust he'll do the same for me. Though I don't mind tellin' you, Sis, I'm sometimes moved to share a word from the Good Book with the 'jacks at the camps. With pastoral duties keepin' the preacher in town most of the week, he can't get out to hold services more'n once in a month of Sundays. So I find myself fillin' in the gap."

"I'd feel better sometimes, Lester, if *you* had a job like that. I–I can't help worrying about you . . . traveling so many miles through the wilderness, roaming from camp to camp for Luke and the Meloney brothers, attending to whatever tasks they find for you to do."

"Aw, there's nothing to worry about. I can take care of myself."

Harmony wasn't convinced. "But misfortune can befall

any mortal, Les. I can't help wondering what might happen with you on foot."

He shrugged. "I can't complain. I'm plenty lucky to have the experience. Why, I've learned more about the lumber business in six months up here than I did in two years back home in Effingham County, logging with Seth Hyatt. But I hope one day to be in business for myself, and all I'm learnin' now will stand me in good stead when I'm ready to strike out on my own."

Harmony frowned. "Still, I worry about your walking the woods alone, Les. There's not only the wild creatures to think about, I've heard the 'jacks talk about Indians, too." Her blue eyes widened. "They've told such terrible tales about raids when the Indians slaughter innocent white settlers and steal small children—heathen practices that are enough to curl your hair. I fear for you, brother, walking about like you do, unable to flee on horseback from man or beast if you're suddenly beset—"

"Harmony, how you do go on. You have a way of stretchin' the facts, you know." Lester chuckled.

"Do I?" she demanded. "This is a harsh and rugged land, Lester Childers. Out here, a small mistake can become a great big tragedy. I don't think you're safe enough afoot. You should be mounted, Les. You don't see your boss, Luke Masterson, walking around!"

"I know. And you're right, Harmony," Lester agreed, "at least, partly. But it can't be helped, Sis. I'd sooner walk on shank's mare than to ride a horse who's lame or been rode too hard. The company can't afford to lose a valuable animal. The horses and oxen work long hours, and I have to watchdog their welfare and stamina . . . even if it means playin' fast and loose with my own."

Harmony gave Lester an impatient look and turned her head toward the window as she stared at the forest, blinking quickly so he would not see her tears of worried frustration. "You, Jeremiah, Alton, and Brad!" she said, sighing heavily. "You're all cut from the same bolt of cloth."

As a small child, she well remembered how her stepfather, Jeremiah, had felt about his mules—even the maverick jack who'd addled his senses and left him with the mind of a little child for the rest of his natural days. Then there was her step-grandfather, Alton Wheeler, who had felt the same way about his team of Clydesdales, Doc and Dan. And Lizzie's third husband, Brad Mathews, who'd been like a pa to both Harmony and Lester, along with his own four motherless daughters. He was partial to horses as well, considering them almost like members of the family, just like Harmon Childers, Lester and Harmony's pa, for whom she'd been named when she was born following his death in a logging accident.

"I might feel different if it was my own mount," Lester said, interrupting her thoughts. "But I'm hired to protect the lumber company's assets as best I can. So I'd rather take my chances on foot than risk the company horses by ridin' them too hard."

"But, Lester," Harmony persisted, "I worry about you spraining your ankle in a groundhog hole or breaking a leg while climbing over a deadfall. There are so many things that could go wrong out there in the woods. Why, you'd be at the mercy of every biting, stinging insect and every wild animal in the territory! And you remember what happened to poor Miss Abby when she wandered away and was exposed to the elements!"

"You worry too much, Sis." Lester tried to dismiss Harmony's dire predictions, even though, truth to tell, he'd shared some of them himself after a near accident or two that could have spelled disaster.

"I can't help it. And don't tell me I'm imagining things, Lester Childers, for I'm not. Kindly remember that I spend my days tending to men who've met up with misfortune. And sometimes it's been the death of them, despite all Dr. Wellingham and I can do. Then we've no choice but to commit their bodily remains to the earth in Pine Hill Cemetery."

"What do you expect me to do?" Lester asked with a trace of irritation in the face of his sister's nagging.

Harmony's gesture expressed the futility she felt. "I don't know. But *something*."

Silence stretched between them for a long moment as the train clattered down the tracks in a soothing cadence.

"Would you feel better to know that I'm plannin' on doin' something about takin' better care of myself, little sister?" He leaned forward in an attitude of supplication.

"Yes," Harmony said, somewhat mollified. But an instant later the tension had returned to her even features. "But what?"

"I've been lookin' to acquire a horse of my own."

"Then obviously you haven't looked very far," she said, her lip curling disparagingly, "or you would have found one by now. There are plenty of horses to be had. . . ."

Lester's jaw jutted forward in a stubborn set. "And some of those animals, my dear sister, I wouldn't have! Why, nobody could *give* me one of those swaybacked, short-winded, flea-bitten, sour-tempered nags!"

"Surely even a decrepit mount would be an improvement over traveling about on your own two legs!"

"That would be debatable," Lester said, his tone benign.

Harmony's face flushed prettily as she turned to face him,

her eyes blazing blue fury. "Don't you put on airs with me, Lester Childers! You could make do with just any old horse for a while and keep a sharp eye out for a proper mount at the same time!"

"I suppose I could . . . but I don't want to," Lester pouted. Then he daydreamed aloud, cataloguing the virtues of the horse of his dreams. "So you see, Harmony, settling for less than that would be saddling myself with disappointment."

Harmony gave a mirthless laugh. "I declare, Les, there are men who'd be less persnickety about finding a woman to wed than you are about a horse!"

Lester grinned, shrugging off the remark.

"As fussy as you are, you'll probably never find a woman, either," Harmony muttered darkly. "I shan't hold my breath. But in case you haven't noticed, there do seem to be plenty of young women in Williams who wouldn't be averse to your coming to court."

"Oh, I've noticed," Lester admitted wearily. "But I'm in the market for a horse, Sis, *not* a wife. You're starting to sound just like Ma, Harmony. Matchmakin' again!"

"Well, you're old enough to think about settling down, Les, and raising a family."

"So are you, Harmony."

"I have my duties at the hospital," she retorted.

"And I have mine with the lumber company!"

Harmony rolled her eyes helplessly. "Luke's right. You *are* married to your job."

"No more than you to your labors of mercy at the hospital."

"That's different."

"Is it? How so?"

"Oh, let's not bicker, Lester," Harmony pleaded.

"We're not bickerin'," he replied. "I was merely posin' a

15

question for which my charming, intelligent, marriageable-aged Florence Nightingale sister has no answer."

"Do promise me you'll find a horse soon," Harmony said, again deftly changing the subject.

"I can promise you I'll find 'im just as soon as the Good Lord sends 'im across my path."

She nodded. "Then I, for one, shall pray that it'll be this very day!"

Lester flashed a dazzling smile. "You'll not hear me complainin'. I've greenbacks in my pocket for just such a deal."

Harmony took heart. "Good. I'd gladly take the train ride back to Williams all by my lonesome if it meant that you were well-mounted." She paused, turning again toward the window. "Les, do you think there'll be horses for sale in Warroad?"

"Wouldn't be surprised. Almost any horse can be bought for the right price. The trick is finding one I'd agree to have."

"What's Warroad like?" Harmony asked, again avoiding what was proving to be a futile discussion. "You've been there and I haven't."

He puzzled over the question for a moment. "It's real different from Williams, even though little more than twenty miles part the two. Warroad is a white man's town now. But before that, it was an Indian village known as Ka-Beck-a-Nung, which means 'end of the trail' in Chippewa, as the Ojibway are now called."

Ka-Beck-a-Nung, located at the mouth of the Warroad River, had been established when the Ojibway migrated to the area in the 1700s, Lester explained. The arrival of the white man eventually followed with the French Voyageurs—Pierre La Verendrye and others attempting to find a route to the West. Instead, they discovered that the wilderness area was rich in fur that could command an attractive price in European cities.

The name given the river and the white man's town—War Road—couldn't have been more appropriate, Lester knew from his understanding of area history, for the wide, deep river was the route used by war parties of both the Sioux and the Ojibway on their way to do battle over the disputed territory. And no doubt other warring tribes had used the same route in centuries preceding the arrival of the bloodthirsty Sioux and the gentle Ojibway.

The tributary that had comprised the natives' road to war ran westward and connected with a trail cut along a gravel ridge that had once formed the shoreline of prehistoric Lake Agassiz. During times of peace, and generally since the arrival of white settlers, the Warroad River and the overland trail had provided a convenient summer route to the west and even to the north, once travelers were able to link up with the Red River.

Warroad, which was well established compared to the much more recent settlement of Williams, had also benefited from lumbering concerns in addition to the fur trade and fishery enterprises. Both the Hudson's Bay Post and the American Fur Company—the latter controlled by John Jacob Astor—had once operated trading posts at the mouth of the river where it entered the mighty Lake of the Woods.

"You'll see many Chippewa braves, their squaws and children on the streets of Warroad, Harmony," Lester warned his sister. "But don't worry. They're plenty friendly when you get to know them."

"Then . . . what I've heard about a possible Indian uprising . . . isn't true?"

Lester shook his head. "Not that I know of. The last time

there was such a rumor, the white folks were quakin' in their boots. True, Indian drums could be heard in the night, but it was no call to war. The natives were simply celebratin' and had no notion that their white neighbors feared for their scalps."

Harmony shuddered. "Imagine what could have happened if the settlers had armed themselves and attacked the Indians first, thinking they were protecting their families!"

"Yep." Lester nodded. "Sorry communication has been at the root of many a tragedy." He leveled an appraising look at his sister. "You might not speak the language, Sis, but when they see that sweet smile of yours, they'll know you have a kind heart and gentle spirit."

She squeezed his hand. "I won't be afraid when I'm with you."

"But I won't be able to be around the whole time," Lester reminded her. "I'm in Warroad on business, remember?"

Harmony nodded, although her features remained a bit troubled, and she lapsed into silence as she regarded a stand of pine that had not known the bite of the ax. "Look how thick the forests are here! Why, Les, a man could take three or four paces into the woods and disappear from sight!"

"True enough. But a woodsman's instincts don't often let him down."

"It appears this land's got enough trees to keep lumbermen cutting forever."

"Lord willin'," Lester said, "that's so. I've never seen such stands of pine . . . prime trees at that. It's a rich bounty, and if tended well, it should yield a rich harvest for many years. But an unexpected disaster . . . and 'jacks would quickly find they'd have sore need to ply a different trade."

"What do you mean?"

Lester's gesture encompassed the mighty trees outside their window. "Seth's talked of woodlands in the Northwest just like these stands. A bolt of lightnin' strikin' ground that's tinder dry, or a stray spark from a locomotive's firebox nestlin' in dry grass and springin' to life, and wildfires have swept whole forests, leavin' nothing but charred devastation. Trees that it could take men decades to fell . . . wiped out overnight."

"What would folks do if that should ever happen?"

Lester squinted in speculation. "Some would undoubtedly move on. But I can't help feelin' pretty hopeful about moving to these parts, Sis, knowin' the settlers hereabouts don't rely solely on the timber. With the Lake of the Woods nearby, there's the fisheries, trapping, farming, ice-harvesting businesses, and other concerns. And there'll always be sick folks for you and Marc to tend to—white settlers and Indians alike."

The train began to slow as they approached a settlement of some kind, and Harmony saw dwellings that apparently belonged to an encampment of local Indians. There seemed to be three styles of housing, with the most common a domed structure.

Lester, noting her interest, explained how the round tepees, or wigwams, were constructed. An inner framework consisted of approximately twenty long poles placed solidly into the ground about two feet apart. Each pole was bent and lashed to the pole directly across from it, forming a roof. Strips of birch bark, cut into sheets and sewn together to make mats, were placed over the skeletal framework and overlapped like shingles. These provided insulation in both summer and winter.

"Inside the dwellings are mats made from cattails sewn

together. If the family decides to move, the birch bark and the cattail rush mats are easily rolled up to take along."

"How interesting. But I think I prefer the accommodations at the Grant Hotel!" Harmony bantered. "And I know I prefer my clothing," she added, spotting some Indians clustered around a tepee.

The small, black-haired children were scantily dressed, and the braves wore only leather breechclouts, while the women were more modestly attired in long skirts and loose shirts. Both men and women wore their hair plaited in long braids and secured with beaded headbands.

At that moment the engineer hauled on the cord and the whistle blew, announcing their arrival in the northern Minnesota border town. The train chugged across the bridge spanning the Warroad River, the massive timbers of the trestle spread like the legs of a sentry standing guard. With the grating sound of steel against steel, the train slowly ground to a halt in front of the depot.

Harmony tied her bonnet securely, collected her reticule, and allowed Lester to steady her as she alit from the coach.

"I'll walk you to the main street of town," he said, "where the businesses are located. You should be able to find what you want easy enough."

"You're a dear, Les," Harmony said, and stood on tiptoes to brush a quick kiss across his cheek. "I do have quite a few items I need to purchase, not only for myself, but for others, too. Marissa and Molly both want flannel yard goods so they can begin sewing layette garments for their coming babes. And Rose Grant, bless her heart, needs some new calico and gingham cloth to sew herself some new dresses." They walked on while Harmony ticked off her plans. Then she paused in contemplation. "You know, Lester, I'd never have dreamed what a heavy woman Rose used to be if I hadn't seen a sepia-toned studio portrait of her taken with her family ten years ago."

"From what Molly said, she dropped the biggest chunk of flesh right after her husband died," he said. "But she's slimmed down a good bit more since we met her in February."

Harmony sighed. "Rose had a kindly face in the photograph. But now it's plain to see that Rose Grant is actually a beauty. I shouldn't be surprised if she remarries eventually."

"There are some of the 'jacks who would like it to be now . . . not 'eventually.'" Lester chuckled.

"Well, she's not interested in them," Harmony said with a sniff.

"That's what I figured, too, but I wasn't sure. Sometimes women can play hard to get, from what I've been told."

"Rose will be choicy if she marries again," Harmony declared. "From bits and pieces I've overheard, I have reason to believe that she wasn't happy with her late husband, God rest his soul."

"Maybe he changed after he married her," Lester said. "Heaven knows I've heard some of the married 'jacks talk about how they wed a female they thought they knew and ended up with a pure stranger!"

"I've heard women complain about the same thing," Harmony pointed out.

Lester shrugged. "Reason enough right there for me to be happy with my state as a confirmed bachelor. At least I can count on myself to be the same day in and day out."

Harmony's blue eyes shone with the excitement of exploring the unusual village with its rich heritage and more to offer than could be found in Williams. Large buildings—a hotel, barber shop, billiard hall, grocery store, rooming house, clothing store, apothecary, and doctor's office located above a drug store—faced the wide street. "Where shall we meet when it's time to depart?" Harmony inquired.

"Reckon I'll be done with my business before you. But if you should finish up early, then you can probably find me over around the livery." He pointed down a side street. "Then we can get a bite to eat at a restaurant before we board the train for home."

"Very well. I'll see you later. And Les, *do* try to find yourself a proper horse. . . ."

He grinned. "It's at the top of my list. For I have a feelin' that the only way to get my devoted sister off my neck is to put me astride the back of a good horse!"

chapter

2

LESTER POLISHED OFF his business for the lumber company, then set out for the livery stable that had been his primary destination since arriving in Warroad. Seeing a group of people standing around outside, he quickened his pace.

A head shorter than most of the others and clean-shaven except for a mustache, Lester stood out in the crowd of bearded woodsmen, trappers, fishermen, and Indians. He wedged his way into the circle of men whose attention was riveted on a rugged trapper, who stood head and shoulders above the rest—*equal in size to the late Alton Wheeler in his prime*, Lester thought.

The man's brawny shoulders were as broad as the length of two ax handles, and his dark brown hair, streaked with gray, hung like a lion's mane on the sweat-stained shoulders of his worn buckskin shirt. His beard, equally unkempt, was matted with grease and particles of food. A portion of the rough thatch was absent, and Lester surmised that the grease-coated whiskers must have caught on fire when the man had either leaned too close to open flames or had tried to ignite the bowl of his pipe with a glowing coal pinched between tongs. "Gather round, boys, for I'm selling her today!" the giant bawled. "For those of you who've hankered to own her . . .

well, here's your chance. So you blokes prepare to put your money where your mouth is. She goes to the highest bidder!"

He gripped in his hand a rein attached to the bridle of a spirited filly's halter. Quickly Lester sized up the beast. She appeared to be about two years old, just the right age to be broken and, if he desired, bred.

As the men moved in closer, the horse nickered nervously and made a skittish sidestep. Then she laid back her dainty, pointed ears and lifted her velvety muzzle into the wind, sniffing danger, as the trapper reined her in.

With a practiced eye, Lester recognized the horse's conformation for what it was, and in his heart he knew she was the horse he'd been waiting for. He had to have her . . . and he'd spend every dime in his pocket, if necessary, to make sure he got her.

"She come to these parts in the belly of her dam," the trapper called out. "Indian tales have it that she's out of prime stock down in Kentucky, she and her dam stole by some savage who come wayfarin' through the region with the tribe.

"She's sound of teeth, solid of bone, and just enough flesh on her to be pleasin'—not so bony as to make a man uncomfortable, and not so fat and sleek that a bloke has to dread the thought of feedin' her through a hard winter. She's a mite young but good for breedin', she be," the trapper said. "Like as not, mated up with the right sire, she'd throw offspring as decent as herself." The trapper paused only long enough to shove a rough wad of tobacco into the bulging indentation of his cheek.

A grizzled woodsman at Lester's side spoke up. "She's a young'un—her chest ain't full developed yet—and her hips ain't bad, if maybe a little skinny for some tastes. But her legs are strong. She'll be able to hold her own in these parts.

Won't straggle or lollygag and tempt a feller to whack her with a stick to convince her to walk a more spritely pace."

"Yessirree!" another man agreed. "She'll be a beauty when she's in her prime . . . another year or so at most."

"I like her colorin', too," said another. "You don't see that burnished copper hue much in these parts."

"She was sired outside the area or, like as not, you'd see some Indian bloodlines in her."

"Might be an interesting combination," Lester thought out loud, having admired Appaloosas and Paints for as long as he could remember.

A man standing nearby gave him a quick, curious look, then offered a hesitant nod as he thought it over. "Might be at that, son," he murmured.

"I'd think Indian blood would give her foals speed and stamina and surefootedness, 'long with that good Kentucky stock," said Lester to support his views.

"Her dam was a good breeder," the trapper said. "Had six or seven afore she died a year ago last spring when she busted through the ice and drownded. Twarn't nothin' no one could do to save her."

Such unfortunate accidents happened yearly, Lester knew, for it was a harsh region and the lake and waterways were the preferred means of transportation for both white man and Indian. There came a time after the water was clogged with ice that easy paddling became impossible and the ice not yet solid enough to support weight. At these times it was dangerous to travel the routes for fear that solid ice would be interspersed with patches of open water, or "rotten" ice, honeycombed with air pockets.

Lester had heard of loggers who had lost their teams of draft horses in the dead of winter when the animals had suddenly plunged through the ice. Sometimes, if the water was shallow, the horses could be hoisted to safety. But if it was too deep, they would slide into the depths and be trapped beneath the surface, unable to find their way back to the narrow opening in the ice.

"I remember it well," a nearby logger grunted. "Turrible accident. She had a young'un at her side. Lost 'em both to the watery depths."

"She was a spirited ol' gal," the trapper said. "Had to watch her, though. Had a temperament and memory to match a mule. She was Jake's equal, that's fer sure. Could've matched him kick for blow . . . iffen she dared. But don't reckon she ever dared take a swipe at ol' Jake. He'd have crowned her 'twixt the ears with a length of stovewood and taught her who's boss.

"The filly's got a plumb nasty glint to her eyes, too. Don't look like a feller better turn his back on her."

"She looks easy-goin' enough to me," Lester observed, drawing the curious stares of the other onlookers.

A lumberjack spoke up. "So what if she's got a stubborn streak? A man could tame that flinty temper soon enough. All it'd take would be a firm hand and she'd be as docile as a tabby cat."

"Right you are!" his friend was quick to agree. "With the proper handlin', she'd be fit for a hard day's work . . . or for a man's pleasure if he took a notion to idle away the hours."

"Well," said another, "good temperament or bad, there's no disagreein' that she's pleasant to the eyes."

The latter observations concurred with Lester's belief, for it appeared that the filly had the lines of a fine saddle horse, perhaps a Tennessee Walker or a bit of quarter horse. *Or*, he thought, his eyes taking the measure of the sorrel horse, *maybe even a little Morgan, enough to make J. P. himself proud.*

"You fellers have had enough time now to look her over. So let's get this show on the road! What'm I bid?" the trapper roared, lifting a stone jug to his lips. Applejack dribbled from the corners of his mouth and ran down his beard as his quick eyes darted over the assemblage, searching for bids, encouraging offers.

A tobacco-chewing 'jack started the bid at what Lester considered an astonishingly low price.

"Tarnation! She be worth more'n that to *me* . . . iffen I have to scratch together the funds or go to my timber boss for an advance agin my pay!" shouted a man at the edge of the circle, and he threw out a higher bid.

The longer Lester looked at the horse, the more he longed to possess her. She was perfect. The only thing that could possibly make her more ideal would be if he knew she was his to own, train, and treasure, his to share with no other man.

When Lester's hand shot into the air, he sensed the eyes of the grizzled lumberjacks upon him, sizing him up.

"What'd *you* do with her?" one asked, his tone a cross between an amused hoot and a sneer. "You don't look seasoned enough to handle a potential spitfire like that 'un! Why, she'd lead you on a merry chase!"

No doubt he appeared suspiciously soft to the hardened lumberjacks and trappers, Lester thought. He knew he was not heavily muscled, for his build was lean and wiry. And seeing him as the timber boss's assistant, instead of doing rugged, manual labor with an ax or two-man saw, they had misjudged his strength.

A few Chippewa braves stood by, mute, their expressions inscrutable, as they took in the situation, missing no detail.

Lester contented himself with the knowledge that they, along with the ragtag assortment of lumberjacks, trappers, and fishery workers, might be in for a surprise if they had any idea how adept he was with horses—or mules! But the tips of his ears flamed to match his cheeks.

The bids went higher and higher, and Lester found himself unable to drop out of the competition. He hung on to the bitter end, even though he knew he'd have only a few dollars left to his name until next payday.

"Sold to the skinny feller in the back row," the trapper announced, "that is, after I see the color of your money, pal!"

"Right here." Lester quickly produced the bills from the worn leather wallet that had been a gift from his mother three Christmases before.

"Well, she's your'n, young feller," the filly's owner said, regret in his tone, as if he wasn't quite sure that the mild-mannered young man could handle his newest acquisition.

"Thanks, mister," Lester said, as he counted out the bills into the giant's outstretched palm. "Now, if you don't mind, I'd like a bill of sale. Iffen I should have to resell her, I'll need legal proof she's mine. For what I've paid for her . . . well, you can understand why I'd want to be sure I owned the filly, free and clear."

The comment brought a riot of laughter from the men, and the trapper roared until he was short of breath as he slapped his thigh and looked around him through eyes crinkled with amusement. "Can you beat that, boys? A bill o' sale he wants!"

"Iffen you don't mind," Lester persisted.

"'Iffen I don't mind,'" the trapper mocked with good-natured bluster and looked around for encouragement. "Well, I don't mind, son. But the fine state o' Minnesota might, so I'll have to decline. By mornin', I'll be long gone from these parts, and I don't plan on leavin' any reasons in writin' for them to hunt me down."

Lester realized that he wanted that horse bad enough to take her with or without a bill of sale, and he contented himself that there were enough people present, including the Chippewa braves, who could testify in his behalf if there was a later dispute. "I'll take her now," Lester said, eager to remove the filly—*his horse*—from the rude reprobate's possession as soon as possible.

"Good luck to you," the bearded trapper said. "Hope you know what you're doin', son. A word of advice: Keep a good grip on her, I warn ye, for she's a handful when she takes the notion."

With that, the man looped the reins around his massive forearm, holding the fiery young horse in a tighter grip. Then, with a motion quicker than the eye could see, he reached around behind him and wrestled forward a young girl of about fifteen, propelling her in Lester's direction.

She staggered ahead, her feet braced until the heels of her moccasin-clad feet dug furrows in the loose sandy soil. Her chin was set in stark defiance and her green eyes blazed with undisguised hatred. Moving erratically, in jerks and forward thrusts, she worked her cheeks and pursed her lips as if considering spitting in Lester's face.

"Thar she be, boy! All your'n! Do with her as you will."

With a jolt the trapper flung the much smaller girl toward Lester, as one might throw a cat at a cornered mouse. She landed with a bone-jarring thud that she didn't bother to acknowledge, but rolled up, springing off the ground on her toes and arising in a stealthy half-crouch. Her matted, auburn hair whipped around her face as she jerked her gaze around the circle of men, as if assessing from which direction danger might arrive next.

The trapper hauled himself up into the saddle, grunting as he settled his bulk astride the poor beast's back. The girl took several staggering steps toward him, her hand outstretched in supplication.

With an angry bellow, the trapper reined in the horse, leaned to port, and backhanded her across the cheek, leaving a crimson mark spreading across her face as she was sent sprawling to the seat of her buckskin britches. The trapper then issued a lightning-fast litany of unfamiliar words that sullied the air. Their meaning, even in the foreign tongue, was clearly hostile as the big man's eyes sparked angrily and his beard bobbed with the intensity of his tirade.

At the torrent of harsh words, the Chippewa braves looked from one to another, their eyes dark pools of horrified disbelief. Stark fear was etched into the girl's wan features. Unbidden, her trembling fingers crept to her throat to clutch a rawhide thong that hung around her neck and disappeared beneath the loose buckskin shirt held together with bone buttons.

With the trapper's hoarse invectives, the life and will to resist seemed to evaporate from the girl's body. Bested, she got to her feet and stumbled obediently toward Lester Childers, head bent low, eyes to the ground. She stood beside him—not close enough for their arms to touch—and remained there, trembling like a whipped pup.

Satisfied, the mounted trapper spat a few more angry words in the unfamiliar tongue, which Lester concluded was the Chippewa dialect. Then he sawed on the reins, jerked the horse's head around, and gouged his heels roughly into her sides.

"Hey! Where do you think you're goin' with my horse?" a shocked Lester screamed after him, sprinting in the direction of the trapper who was riding off on the beautiful animal. "Come back here! That's *my filly!*" But Lester's legs were no match for the horse's speed.

"That there's the filly you bought, you young fool!" the trapper called out with a backward glance. "This here four-legged filly's mine . . . and she ain't for sale at any price!"

"Oh, dear Lord . . ." Lester murmured, stunned as the impact of the duplicitous transaction hit him with full force.

Shaken, almost blind with anger and helplessness, he turned back to face the group of men who were almost rolling on the ground in amusement.

"Y–you didn't buy a horse, you young whippersnapper. What you just did was up and buy yourself a woman! And a plenty nice one, too. Iffen you don't mind sellin' her at a loss, you can pawn her off in a matter of minutes by conductin' your own auction."

For a moment, Lester was sorely tempted. But as he eyed the dejected stance of the young woman, who looked as if she'd spent her entire lifetime doing another's bidding, he knew he couldn't do it. Even though his baser instincts cried out to him to recoup his losses, his Christian convictions would never allow for it. "Dear Lord," he sighed under his breath, "whatever am I goin' to do?"

Lester stood rooted to the spot, trying to think as the trappers, loggers, and fishermen—their afternoon's entertainment at an end—drifted away.

Harmony found him there a few minutes later. "Lester . . . what's wrong? You're pale as a ghost!"

"I was snookered!" he said, his voice cracking. "Taken in like a greenhorn rube!"

"Snookered?" she echoed dully. Her older brother was an intelligent fellow, keen and far-thinking. It wasn't like him to be easily taken in. "What happened, Les?"

"I found the horse I wanted . . . the horse of my dreams."

When he began to describe the animal to her, she recognized it as the treasure Lester had long been awaiting. "But what happened?"

"I had the winning bid," he said, then he laughed, a strange sound somewhere between a chuckle and a sob.

"If you had the winning bid . . ." Harmony's eyes widened and she looked all about her, "then where's your horse?"

"The seller rode off on her!"

Harmony's mouth dropped open. "You mean he took your money . . . and then rode off on the very horse he'd just auctioned for sale?"

"Yes! Except it wasn't the *horse* he was sellin', Harmony, it was *her!*" Lester spun about, jabbing his thumb in the direction of the defiant young woman in smelly buckskins.

Fiery red hair fanned about her shoulders in a riotous tangle. There was a smudge of dirt on her cheek, and her nails were broken and dirty. Through her worn moccasins, the girl's toes dug into the sand as if she were attempting to root herself to the spot where she stood, lest she be carried away against her will.

"Oh, Lester!" Harmony breathed, appalled at the wretched apparition.

"Everyone else knew what was goin' on. But I was so intent on negotiatin' the deal that it never occurred to me that trader was actually puttin' a woman on the auction block! Why, the way he was describin' that girl . . . she sounded just like the horse!"

32

"Then you paid a high price, didn't you?" Harmony sympathized.

"All but a few dollars to last me 'til payday," he admitted.

"Oh, Lester, I'm so sorry!"

"Fool me once, shame on you. Fool me twice, shame on *me*," he said in a tired tone. "But it'll never happen again. I'll be a whole heap wiser for this experience." He sighed heavily. "Come on, Sis, let's go catch the train. We can get a few sandwiches at the restaurant to eat in the coach on the ride home. And please don't say anything to anyone about this when we get back to Williams, will ya? If the 'jacks ever get wind of this . . . I'll never live it down."

Lester took a few purposeful steps in the direction of the depot when Harmony's words halted him. "Les, what are we going to do?"

He kept walking. "We're going home to Williams, that's what."

"Lester Childers, you turn around here right now! I'm asking you what we're going to do . . . with *her!*"

He turned reluctantly, his eyes glazed. "An hour ago, she wasn't my concern . . . and an hour from now, she won't be, either."

"Lester, we can't just leave her here in the street, for heaven's sake! This girl has just been abandoned. Sold! Think what would happen to her if we left her!"

"I've seen mules with a sweeter disposition, Harmony. Trust me, that little heathen spitfire can fend for herself. She may be small, but she's got the strength of several men. I have a hunch she can give as good as she'd get. Don't worry, Sis. She can take care of herself."

"I'm grateful Mama's not here to hear you talk like this, Lester Childers, or our pa, either. You knew our pa, and I didn't, but everyone's said Harm Childers was a kind and gentle man, one who'd put himself out to help someone in trouble."

He flinched. "Ouch! You really know how to hurt a fellow, Harmony."

Lester was torn. On one hand, he wanted to walk away as fast as he could in the opposite direction; on the other, he was drawn to the pitiful wretch he saw before him, wanted to get her to a safe place before going on with his own life. "You've made your point, Harmony. But I'm at a loss as to what to do. Any suggestions?"

Harmony's winged brows came together in a frown. "Well, we can't leave her here," she mused. "We'll simply have to take her back to Williams . . . with us!"

"No!" Lester cried, his eyes sparking. "I won't be made the laughingstock of the whole town."

"Hmph! What do you care what they say when the life of this poor girl is at stake? Would you consign her to more misery, with no one to protect her, no one to care?"

Lester pinched his eyes shut and turned away, unwilling to gaze on the pitiful child. But there was no need. For his mind was already rife with awful imaginings of what her lot would be if abandoned to the mercy of a town that might prove to have no mercy. He had been in the town often enough to know that he wouldn't wish such an outcome on his worst enemy, let alone a girl who was as much a victim of the trapper's scheme as he.

"All right then, we'll take her to Williams with us," Lester said. "But she's *your* responsibility. I may have accidentally purchased her, Harmony, but as of this moment, I'm givin' her to *you!*"

"I'm beholden to your generosity, brother," said Harmony

with a hint of sarcasm. "At least in me she'll know she has a friend. . . ."

"It's not that I dislike her, Sis," Lester protested. "It's just that I wanted a *horse!*"

"It's a curious situation, Les, that I'll grant you. But even so, I draw comfort and direction from the fact that the Lord doesn't make mistakes. I know that even when things look terribly, terribly wrong, in the end he'll make sure it all turns out exactly right."

In response, Lester gave a short, disbelieving laugh. With his disappointment high, his funds low, and his mortification complete, his own faith did not stretch that far.

Minutes later, the trio traveled in silence toward the depot. On the way, they stopped at the restaurant long enough to purchase three ham sandwiches prepared with thick slices of perfectly cured pork between solid slabs of fresh baked bread, wrapped in waxed paper.

En route to the train, Lester took the lead, followed by Harmony, with the reluctant girl trailing in their wake. With smiles of encouragement and gestures she hoped would be understood, Harmony urged her along.

"Les, I need a favor," Harmony murmured when they reached the depot.

He gave an impatient glance over his shoulder. "Now what?"

"Since I'm responsible for her, I'll need another ticket." She motioned toward their companion. "If you'll loan me the money, I'll repay you when we get back to Williams."

With a snort of disgust, Lester threw down the money at the ticket counter. "Just forget it," he ordered in a glum tone. "If I'm in for a dime, may's well be in for another dollar." He surveyed the empty slot in his wallet and drew no comfort that only a few coins remained to jingle in his pocket.

"I've heard tell of blokes who went broke over pleasurable involvements with women," he went on, "but I never thought such a plight would befall me . . . and all on account of a filthy, smelly, nasty-eyed girl who's bound to be a source of aggravation to anyone unfortunate enough to cross her path!"

"I think she has real possibilities, Les," Harmony murmured as they took facing seats on the train—she and Lester sitting across from the sullen white-Indian girl. "A hot bath and the generous application of a scrub brush to elbows, feet, and ears will do wonders for her."

Lester made no reply but adjusted his hat lower on his forehead, feigning disinterest and a desire to sleep.

"Her hair's a mess now," Harmony mused, studying the features of their reluctant traveling companion. "But several good latherings with lye soap and some verbena-scented rinse water will make a world of difference."

Lester kept his own counsel.

"But those buckskins have got to go," his sister continued. "I think she's probably about my size. Surely I have something she can wear until we can make some proper garments for her."

Lester could stand it no longer. "Harmony, do you have any notion what you're gettin' yourself into?"

"I'm prepared to see to it that she's bathed and clothed, with a roof over her head and food in her stomach, until I can figure out what to do with her. Why, it's our Christian duty, Lester. Maybe Marissa, Molly, and Rose will have some ideas." Harmony paused in thought. "Speaking of food . . . I'm hungry. Shall we eat?"

Lester, who had lost his appetite along with his money, handed over the waxed paper bundle of sandwiches.

"One for you . . ." Harmony counted them out, "one for me, and one for our . . . new friend." She handed the girl a sandwich, indicating that it was hers and that she should eat.

The girl stared at the food, then at Harmony, who took a dainty bite and chewed slowly. Clutching the thick sandwich in her grimy hands, the girl stared at it for a long moment. Then, apparently ravenous, she bit off huge chunks, chewed once or twice, and bolted it down, bite after large bite, until it was gone.

"Heavens to Betsy!" Lester gasped, appalled by the gluttonous display. "How long can it be since she's had anything to eat?"

His own sandwich rested, untasted, on the waxed paper on his lap. He placed it in front of Harmony. "Give it to her," he said. "The poor wretch is starvin'."

"But aren't you hungry?"

"No, I'm too sick with misery to eat. If my appetite returns by the time we get back to Williams, I'll go by the hotel and have Rose fix me a bite . . . that is, if my credit's still good there. . . ."

"Maybe your faith is being put to the test, Les. Doesn't the Lord tell us in the Good Book that when we do for the least among us, we're doing for him?"

As Lester mulled over his sister's remark, he felt a fleeting moment of hope in what had thus far been a dark and despairing day. And even as his stomach began to growl with hunger, there was a good feeling even in the emptiness within.

"Here we are!" Harmony said when the train slowed to a halt in front of the depot in Williams an hour later.

Lester arose, shaking the stiffness from his joints.

"Poor thing fell asleep," Harmony said, gesturing toward the girl. "I'll have to wake her. Miss . . . miss," she called softly, touching the girl's forearm.

The green eyes flickered, hooded with slumber, then flashed open, instantly alert. Her body tensed and she lashed out at Harmony instinctively.

Instead of recoiling, however, Harmony stretched out her hand in a gesture Lester recognized. It was the same move he'd made many times to gentle a frightened animal—letting it catch his scent and grow accustomed to the idea of his presence.

Slowly, slowly, Harmony's hand moved toward the girl who seemed poised to spring, and touched the matted hair. "Come," she whispered. She took the grimy hand and motioned for her to rise. "Come along now. We're going home."

Harmony's grip was firm but kind as she hauled the still reluctant girl down the aisle toward the door leading from the coach. For a moment Lester was afraid he might have to apply his shoulder to the seat of her buckskins to convince her to step from the coach onto the siding, scarcely visible in the dusky evening light.

"Mark my words, she's going to be a real *joy* for you to live with, Harmony," Lester warned. "I hope you haven't bit off more than you can chew and aren't going to rue the day you took on this . . . this heathen."

"Joy!" Harmony breathed the word, her gleeful tone cutting off Lester's litany of worry. "*That's* what we'll call her . . . *Joy!*"

"Call her Joy," Lester grunted. "Folks are goin' to be callin' you 'Crazy', and me 'Fool.'"

"I don't mind being a fool for the Lord," Harmony said

happily. "And God willing, with his help and ours, maybe someday this poor heathen girl will live up to her new name!"

Lester cast her a dubious glance. "That would take a miracle."

"With God," Harmony reminded him, "all things are possible. Why," she teased, "you might even fall in love with our Joy!"

"Now that's the most addlepated thing you've *ever* said, Harmony Childers!" Lester hotly protested, moving farther out of range.

"Oh . . . I don't know about that," she teased, glancing at the scowling girl who was glaring at her big brother, "I think she's beginning to be attracted to you. Given time, she might even come to like you."

"Then she's wastin' her time," Lester sputtered, "for I'd die happy if I never saw the wretched creature again!"

Even as he spoke the words, Lester Childers knew he didn't mean one of them. It was as if the vision of the wild and impetuous Joy had been branded in his mind forever. Even when he was not looking, her image remained—strong and spirited and with hair flowing wild and free like the sorrel horse of his dreams. . . .

chapter
3

AFTER THEY DISEMBARKED from the Canadian National train, Lester accompanied Harmony and the girl his sister had named Joy through the side streets of Williams. He was painfully aware of the curious stares they drew from the town's few residents who were out and about at that time of evening, and he felt his face redden to the tips of his ears when he detected the buzz of whispered comments that followed in their wake.

At the corner, Harmony accepted the offer of Lester's arm to help her across the rutted road. Out of habit, he extended the same courtesy to their grimy companion.

The girl tossed back her matted red hair and gave him what he could only construe as a hostile glance. She jerked herself away from Lester, recoiling as if from a red-hot stove, then apparently thinking better of it, reluctantly allowed him to assist her. But her arm beneath his fingertips was rigid, enduring his touch only for the brief moment necessary to steady her steps.

Finding himself suddenly downwind of the girl, Lester realized that the first order of business before she could be settled into the Wellingham home—if only on a temporary basis—was a bath. He couldn't help smiling to himself as he envisioned the scenario when Marissa and Harmony tried coaxing the girl into a tub of warm, soapy water, scented with cologne. He suspected that it would require brute force, not gentle feminine persuasion.

From what the trapper had said, Lester wasn't too sure that the strong, wiry redhead might not be more than a match for Harmony and Marissa combined. And even Dr. Wellingham, if called into the fray, might be hard-pressed to subdue the little spitfire. Well, Lester was glad he could soon wash his hands of her and leave her to the women's ministrations.

Nearing the Wellingham home, Harmony's steps quickened. But Lester was too tired, disappointed, and broke to stick around for Marissa's reaction to the arrival of an unexpected houseguest. As children on the banks of Salt Creek in Illinois, he well remembered her volatile nature when displeased. Still, over the past few months, he'd noticed many changes in Marissa Wheeler, now Wellingham, the girl who could have so easily claimed his heart long ago if she had but taken the time to notice him.

A few minutes later, with his sister and her unkempt charge safely deposited on the front stoop of the Wellingham home, Lester turned on his heel and quickly fled down the few steps to the street, where he retraced his path.

Checking his timepiece as he strode along the sidewalk in front of the Grant Hotel, the grumbling of his stomach overrode the near emptiness of his pockets. With a sigh he mounted the steps of the hotel, opened the massive front door, and trudged toward the dining room where Widow Grant and her growing girls would soon be closing up for the night. Maybe it wasn't too late to get a little something to tide him over until morning.

"Well, hello, Lester!" Rose sang out a warm greeting.

"Evenin', Rose." He doffed his hat, managing to muster a tired smile as he slid into the chair she held for him.

"A long day tradin' in Warroad?"

"Too long."

"Successful, I hope," she chirped as she bustled about the table, unfolding his napkin and laying it in his lap.

"Harmony found everything she'd set out to purchase for herself and half the womenfolk in town, it seemed to me. I know she was right pleased with the fabric she brought you, Rose. Expect she'll hie on over here with it first thing in the morning. . . ." He paused. "That is, unless you'd like to hurry down to Wellinghams' and pick it up for yourself."

"I might just do that," Rose said, patting her hair into place, "as soon as I serve you. The girls can do up the dishes without me."

"Harmony'll be up for a while," Lester said, thinking of the ordeal she would soon be facing with the half-wild girl.

Rose gave him a calculated glance. "Hope you located what *you* were looking for today, Lester."

Lester was silent for a long moment as the events of the day spiraled through his mind. "Reckon I got way more than I'd bargained for. . . ."

"How wonderful!" Rose replied, so caught up in her own secret joy that she failed to detect his tone of abject misery.

"What's on the menu tonight, Rose?"

"All your favorites, Lester," she replied with a lilt in her tone.

He tossed down the sheet listing the day's offerings. "Just bring me a big plate of whatever you have left. I'm not fussy. You're like Ma. Anything you fix tastes good."

"The stew's right tasty, if I do say so myself, and hard to beat with rolls fresh from the warmin' oven." She took another look at him. "It's comin' right up, just as soon as I fetch a cup of strong black coffee. You look like you could use a mug of brew to revive your senses."

She left for the kitchen with an unaccustomed bounce in her step and returned with a big granitewear pot and a cut glass creamer and sugar bowl nestled in her other hand. "There you go!" she said and, with a grand flourish, filled the heavy mug.

"You're a gem, Rose," Lester said and gratefully raised the stoneware cup to his lips and took a sip.

"It would seem that *some* folks think so," Rose said, sounding unusually pleased. "And I'm honored that you're among that number." She cocked her eye at him. "I reckon you're aware that we have a new face in Williams, someone newly arrived?"

Lester's pleasant respite was banished with this reminder of his distressing day. "That I am," he said, feeling annoyed with Rose's delight in having spied the arrival of the grubby stranger. He was grateful when she didn't question him further but left to tend to his order in the kitchen.

A minute or two later she reappeared with a steaming plate of stew, chunky with potatoes, carrots, and cubes of tender beef swimming in a savory gravy. "A plate of stew . . . rolls . . . and a side of coleslaw to round out the meal," she said, placing the dishes before him. "And a big slab of my famous apple pie . . . on the house! I feel like celebratin' myself tonight!"

"Well, thanks, Rose," Lester said, thinking of the dwindling funds in his pocket. "Until you're better paid."

"Just enjoy it, son, that's all I ask." Rose gave him a warm pat on the shoulder as she passed by. "Now I think I'll put on a light wrap and carry these old bones over to the hospital to collect that fabric you mentioned. As of today, I've some grand plans for that material, I have!"

Lester stared into his plate as the Widow Grant made her way out the front door, loathe to spoil her fine mood with news of what awaited her at the physician's house.

He ate steadily, relishing the hot, perfectly seasoned food, wiping up gravy with a crust of roll before turning his attention toward the pie. When he had eaten the last bite, he pushed back his plate and supped his coffee that had been reheated by a blushing Becky. Seeing her so flustered, Lester realized that Rose Grant's eldest daughter was likely one of the young hopefuls Harmony had had in mind when she'd mentioned the romantic possibilities in Williams. Not wanting to encourage the simpering girl, Lester settled up his bill, left a coin on the table for a gratuity, then made his way out into the starlit night.

Off in the distance, across the tracks, emanating from the direction of the Black Diamond Saloon, the sharp report of a gunshot rent the air. Lester paused, waiting, expecting another. But it did not come. He shrugged. Perhaps it was only a random shot, some inebriated 'jack or trapper drawing his shooting iron in protest of the turn of a card or out of jealousy over a tavern girl's attentions to another. A moment later peace had settled over the small town once more, with only the sound of an owl softly hooting and the chirping of crickets to disturb the hush of evening.

Instead of going directly home to his quarters, Lester found himself walking past his corner and on to the Wellingham residence two blocks away. As he drew near, the place seemed peaceful, a lamp winking through the window was the only sign of life. Lester was about to believe he had misjudged the situation when he heard a muffled cry, then an angry yowl, alternating with syncopated squeals of dismay.

"Yup! They're givin' the wretch a bath," Lester whispered to himself, unable to suppress an amused grin. "And from the sounds of things . . . she's not takin' to it like a duck to water."

If anything, he suspected that Joy was resisting with all the fighting savvy of the best Chippewa warrior, for that's what she'd reminded him of—a white-skinned Indian! No doubt, the color of her skin was the *only* similarity between the girl and the well-bred young women of his acquaintance.

Joy, the white Indian, was undoubtedly getting the scrubbing of her life. He found himself idly wondering what she would look like, scoured clean, her hair shampooed and scented, her lean, lithe body dressed in Harmony's garments. But with all their best efforts, there was nothing that could be done about that mulish glint in Joy's eyes, a cast that reminded him of the maverick jackass who'd kicked Jeremiah Stone in the head and addled his senses.

Jeremiah, Ma's second husband, had been challenged to tame the beast with kind treatment, though Alton Wheeler had snorted that he was nothing but "the Devil's spawn." Lester now wondered if kind treatment could temper the fierce-eyed white-Indian girl, or if she, too, was "the Devil's spawn."

Had Joy been a stubborn horse instead of a recalcitrant young woman he himself might have been duped into trying his hand at taming her spirit. "But if anyone can work a miracle with that heathen, same as I'm able to do with horseflesh," Lester muttered under his breath, "it'd be my sister Harmony, with the likes of Marissa, Rose, and Molly standin' by, if need be. God help them all!"

45

Content to leave things in the women's capable hands, he pivoted around and set off in the opposite direction, Joy's furious cries still piercing the night.

Lester had just come abreast of the Grant Hotel again on his way home, his footfalls echoing in the darkness, when a masculine voice called out, "That you, Rose darlin'?"

Before Lester could respond, there was the creak of the porch glider as someone arose and came down the front steps.

"Sorry to disappoint you, sir," Lester said, not recognizing the tall, well-dressed stranger, "but I'm not the one you're lookin' for. Mrs. Grant is still at the Wellingham place . . . and I wouldn't be surprised if she'll be there for quite some time."

"Pardon my mistake, son," the man said, and there was a hint of rueful laughter in his tone. "I came down from my quarters in the hotel and the girls told me their mama had left for a spell. Thought I'd sit here and wait for her to get back. We have a lot of catching up to do." He stuck out his hand. "The name's Homer Ames. And who might you be?"

"Lester Childers."

"Lester! Well, how do you do! Rose can't say enough about you and your family," the older man went on. "Since I arrived from the west on the midday train, she's filled me in on almost every citizen of the town. She holds you, your sister, and your folks back in Illinois in the highest esteem."

"And we think Rose Grant is a mighty fine woman . . . the best." Lester eyed the man suspiciously.

"Yes, I've known Rose since we were tadpoles. From my view, to know Rose is to love her."

Lester relaxed a little, quirking a brow. "So it's Rose you're here to see."

"Actually, I'm here on business, the banking business.

Though, I must say, the idea that this is Rose's home gave added luster to the notion of a business trip."

"We could use a bankin' establishment in Williams," Lester responded thoughtfully.

"My sentiments, exactly," Homer said. "And I believe I can convince my associates of a need for expansion."

"If that happens, would you be the bank official in charge?"

The man pursed his lips. "Perhaps in a few years, though for now, my services are required at the main bank in Fargo. I'll have to return there soon . . . much sooner than I'd like. And when I go, I'd like to know that Rose will eventually be joining me."

The idea of Rose leaving Williams struck Lester like a blow. In the few months he'd known the woman, he'd come to look on her as the very spirit of the town, the epitome of all that its citizens should be. "Then your gain would be our loss," he said hesitantly.

"Oh, I wouldn't take her away for long. It's my intention that we settle here permanently," Homer Ames explained. "Trust me, son. As one who's had to live apart from Rose Grant all these many years, I'd not deny others the delight of her company."

"Well then, it's been nice meetin' you, sir," Lester said heartily. "Perhaps our paths will cross again before you leave for home."

"Knowing Rose, I think we can count on it."

Almost no sooner had Harmony closed the door to the Wellingham residence behind Joy and herself than the full impact of her dilemma struck her. Maybe Lester was right. What did she know about caring for a half-grown woman, an uncivilized one at that! Suddenly she felt overwhelmed by the enormity of her rash decision.

But Marissa proved to be a great comfort when she came in from the kitchen to greet them. As a physician's wife, Harmony's former neighbor had already confronted all manner of unusual cases and was not easily rattled. Upon hearing the bizarre tale, she managed a weak but welcoming smile.

"Oh, you can speak freely," Harmony invited. "She seems to understand absolutely no English. Lester thinks she was probably brought up by Indians."

Marissa shook her head in stunned disbelief. "Heavens! She looks like something the cat dragged in," she admitted, uttering the words sweetly so that the sullen-faced girl would not be able to translate by the tone of her voice. "And smells like it, too! I should think a bath is in order. Fortunately, there's a reservoir full of hot water in the wood range."

While the two women talked, the girl's eyes darted from one face to the other, her stance unyielding.

"She doesn't appear to be the cooperative sort," Marissa observed. "Better keep an eye on her while I fill the tub with water and fetch the linens and soap. I have an idea she's not going to shuck out of those filthy buckskins without a fight."

"Oh, I don't think she'll try to escape," Harmony assured her. "But from what Lester said, she's accustomed to defending herself and may not understand we wish her no harm. No doubt she was treated like a squaw, so she's plenty tough. He told me that the Chippewa womenfolk do pretty much all that the men do, from dressing the kill from the hunts to tanning the hides and hauling heavy loads, and all that while carrying their papooses on their backs!"

Marissa eyed the girl with growing suspicion. "I wish Molly were here to lend us a hand. I can see we're going to have our hands full." She set her lips in a line of gentle determination. "Are we ready to begin?"

"I'm game whenever you are."

Joy, sensing her fate, edged away warily, though there was nowhere for her to go.

The two women closed in.

Harmony eased herself toward Joy, soothing her as Lester would have a skittish colt. "Easy . . . easy now. You'll feel ever so much better when you're nice and clean."

Joy tried to back up, but a sideboard prevented her retreat. Her green eyes darted this way and that as she looked for an avenue of escape but found none.

"Watch her!" Marissa cried.

The shrill sound startled the girl, who had been mute throughout the evening and, like a trapped animal, she stood poised, ready to flee.

"Don't let her get away!" Harmony warned.

"I've got her!" Marissa grabbed at the buckskin shirt. A worn leather fringe, rotting from a combination of grime, age, and sweat, snapped off in her fingers as Joy roughly shoved her away. Marissa went kiting in one direction while Joy scrambled desperately in another.

Then the girl faced them, feet planted wide apart, in the stance of an Indian fighter, daring the women to approach.

"What are we going to do now?" Harmony whispered helplessly.

With a determined swipe of her hand, Marissa brushed her hair from her face, and with a huff through her lips, blew her bangs away from her brow. "What we're going to do is give the little heathen the lathering of her life, even if we fall into the tub with her!"

Harmony almost laughed, for at that moment she could

see that Marissa Wheeler Wellingham was very much Alton's daughter, possessing the same flinty determination that had seen her pa through so many trials and tribulations. "But how are we ever going to coax her out of her clothes?"

"First time through the water," Marissa said, "I have a feeling we won't. I'm going to shove on her, Harmony, and you grab an arm and haul her along. We'll push her into the tub fully clothed. My stomach's been plumb flighty with the coming babe as it is, and I can't take much more of her stench."

"If you think that's what we should do . . ." Harmony moved into position.

"I do! And here goes!" Marissa declared, heaving in behind Joy, who was about her height, though not as well-nourished.

Joy braced her moccasin-clad feet against the hardwood floor. But already a film of moisture had gathered from the effects of the steam, and the smooth leather skimmed onward as if she were on ice skates.

"We're almost there!" Harmony said.

Joy, realizing that the steaming vat of water was their intended destination for her, let out a cry like a brave's war whoop and resisted with every fiber of her being.

With Harmony tugging, Marissa shoving, and Joy balking, inch by inch the trio progressed toward the aluminum tub brimming with hot, soapy water. As Harmony tried to lever Joy into the water, her foot slipped and she fell heavily. Off balance, Joy catapulted forward with a scream. Reaching out, clawing for anything with which to steady herself, her grasping fingers came into contact with Harmony's full skirt, and she toppled into the water, a death grip on the cotton calico dress.

Harmony struggled against the awkward tug, lost the battle, and fell backward, flopping into the tub on top of Joy, whose screams became a burbled croak as her head was driven beneath the surface. A tidal wave of water splashed in all directions, sluicing across the floor and creating a massive puddle that spread out in the room.

At the very moment Harmony and Joy pitched into the tub, Marissa found herself shoving at thin air. She tried to counter the forward momentum, but the sudden flood of soapy water on the hardwood floor thwarted her efforts and she slid ahead, thrashing, her arms flailing, as she fell headlong, landing half in, half out.

Wallowing about, Harmony hefted herself off Joy and over the rim of the tub, collapsing in a sodden heap on the floor as Joy continued to struggle to regain her footing.

"Don't let her get out!" Marissa bawled. "She can't fight near as hard in the tub as she can out of it!"

The ordeal took longer than the pair of women had expected, and they were panting from exertion, their dresses wetly plastered to their bodies before they had cleansed the first appendage. Grabbing a slippery arm, Harmony applied lye soap and a washcloth to the grubby surface, only to have Joy jerk away. As her limb disappeared under the frothy water, they reached for another.

Eventually, Joy's struggles grew weaker, her protests less vocal.

"I think we can finally wrestle the buckskins from her without risking life and limb," Marissa puffed, reaching for Joy's right foot and peeling a sodden moccasin from it. "Heavens! Her feet are still as dirty as if she'd walked through a hog swill barefoot! Grab her other foot, Harmony, and scour hard between those toes!"

They hauled on Joy's legs, which made her shoulders sink into the depths, and she let out a scream of terror.

"Be quick about it, 'Rissa!" Harmony cried. "I can't hold her much longer."

Marissa dropped Joy's newly cleaned foot into the tub with a splash. The girl floated limply for a moment, her features glazed with exhaustion.

"I think the fight's gone out of her enough now that we can shuck that stinky shirt off her," Marissa said. "Take it by the cuff and let's peel it off. You work with one sleeve . . . I'll take care of the other."

Harmony and Marissa knotted their fingers into the wet leather and tugged against its damp resistance as the wet hide shirt stubbornly clung to Joy's skin. Slowly they stripped the filthy garment off. With a triumphant cry, Marissa tossed it to the floor with a wet, flopping smack.

Joy wailed all the louder and tried to cover herself with her arms as Marissa grabbed a bath brush and went to work on her back as Harmony doused shampoo into her hair and ladled water over her until the girl choked and sputtered.

Not once did Joy release her grip on a leather thong around her neck from which hung what appeared to be a medicine bag. Maybe the girl believed it possessed protective powers, even if at the moment it was failing to provide immunity from Harmony and Marissa's ministrations.

When the bathwater became brackish, so dirty that the bubbles died away, Marissa took note. "We'll have to rinse her off with clean water," she gasped. "And maybe we can bend her over the washtub and give that mop of hair another soaping. . . ."

"I don't know if I can hold her," Harmony admitted.

"You *have* to! We can't stop now!"

Just then they heard a knock at the door.

"Tarnation!" Marissa flared. "Someone's at the door!" Sucking in her breath, she called, "Come on in . . . the door's open."

There was a creak in the parlor and then the kitchen door whined open a crack. "Anyone home?" Rose Grant called out from behind the partially closed door.

"Thank God, it's you, Rose!" the two women cried in unison.

"We can use your help," Marissa begged. "We're giving a young savage the bath of her life."

Rose carefully entered the room that was awash with water, steamy from the humidity, and littered with piles of wet clothes and discarded towels.

"We *think* there's a girl under all of this," Marissa said, "and you're just in time to help us find out, Rose. Lend a hand, if you would, for Harmony and I are both plumb tuckered out. . . ."

Carefully Rose picked her way across the floor and laid a calm hand on Joy's upper arm. The girl recoiled from her touch, although she was too exhausted to do more than put up a feeble struggle.

"There, there, child, I won't hurt you," Rose assured.

Joy's glassy stare revealed a total lack of comprehension.

"She doesn't understand English," Marissa muttered as she applied a towel to her own damp blond hair.

"The best we can tell, Rose, this girl was raised by the Chippewas as one of their own," Harmony explained.

Rose hesitated a moment, seeming to collect her thoughts, then she began to speak slowly, haltingly, as if struggling to recall words that were foreign to Marissa and Harmony.

Joy's eyes widened in amazement. Then she faced Rose and began to gibber in a torrent of Chippewa, seeming to believe that in Rose Grant she'd found a benefactor. She accepted the towel the woman extended to her and, with a glare over her shoulder at Marissa and Harmony, slipped from the tub and stood shivering as Rose piled more towels around her.

Smoothing her tangled tresses, Rose spoke a few words in Chippewa, conveying to Joy that her hair was still dirty and that, if she'd agree, Rose would like to finish the job.

Seconds ticked off on the grandfather clock in the nearby hallway, seeming to mark an eternity.

"Ayuh. . . ." Joy agreed.

Marissa and Harmony kept their distance as Rose led the girl to the washtub, humming softly as she located the shampoo, the pitcher of water, and a new supply of towels, occasionally saying a word or two in Chippewa that seemed to appease the frightened young woman.

"We'll have to hope that Doc Wellingham has no call to do surgery this evening," Rose mused, "for we've certainly raided his linen closet this night." She gestured at the discarded towels, hastily strewn about on the floor to soak up the deluge of bathwater slopped over the sides of the tub.

"There are more where those came from," Marissa replied.

"And here's me hopin' the good physician won't need 'em. But as I was mountin' the stoop to knock on your door, I heard the report of gunfire. Sounded like it came from that den of iniquity across the tracks."

Marissa sighed. "That place is a blight upon the landscape, a regular scourge of the town. Keeps Marc busy stitching up knife wounds or treating gunshot victims. But when he became a physician, he vowed to bring healing to one and all . . . and that includes those injured through their own folly."

"Those 'jacks and trappers are a tough lot," Rose acknowledged, vigorously lathering Joy's hair. "If a bloke was just winged, like as not, we'll not hear from him. But iffen he was hurt bad enough to conclude he needs a doctor, he's probably closer to needin' an undertaker! We can only hope the fellow who squeezed off the shot wasn't in any condition to shoot true."

When Rose had applied rinse water until it ran clear, she asked Marissa, "Could you fetch me a spot of vinegar? It cuts the natural oils and gives a shine to the tresses."

"Coming right up!" Marissa said and extracted a brown stone jug from the cabinet. Removing the cork stopper, she then poured several glubs of vinegar into the pitcher before refilling it with pleasantly warm water.

"I've got some verbena cologne in my room," Harmony said, "It'll take away the vinegar smell. I'll go get it. Be right back."

When Harmony returned with the atomizer of scent, she appeared agitated. "There's a commotion on the street!" she announced as she rushed back into the room. "I don't know what it's all about . . . but from the sound of things, it doesn't bode well. I'm afraid someone was hurt in that shooting, Rose."

"Heavens! We've got to get this poor girl out of the altogether before some of the town's menfolk come callin'," Rose said, dashing the pitcher of water over Joy's long tresses with little preamble, leaving the girl choking over the moisture and fumes.

"Grab a comforter from the bedroom," Marissa instructed Harmony. "Wrap her in it and take her to your quarters while I answer the door."

Marissa was tucking wet tendrils of hair behind her ears, shivering from the wet garments that clung to her body, as she peered through the oval glass of the front door. In the dim glow created by the porch lamp, she could see that it was Marc. Behind him, two gigantic lumberjacks supported a much smaller man between them. The man, dark-haired and swarthy-complected, hunched forward, doubled over in pain.

Grateful that she didn't have to open the door and invite the men in to await the doctor's attention, Marissa rushed to the master bedroom so she could make herself presentable as Rose dried and dressed Joy and Harmony made her own repairs.

"Bring the patient into my operating room," Marissa heard her husband call out to the congregation of loggers. "And you boys hang around to help hold him while I remove the bullet."

Harmony, who had also overheard Marc's instructions to the lumberjacks, rushed to assist the doctor, and Marissa hurried to be of use, too.

Aware of her bedraggled condition, Marissa nonetheless held her head high as she swept past the knot of lumberjacks who doffed their grimy hats out of respect for her. "Is there anything I can do to help, Marc?"

Glancing up at her, he quirked a brow in surprise. "Yes, there is. You can get to bed at once, my dear, before you need a doctor yourself. I won't have you risking our wee one's life to keep this rapscallion's body and soul together."

"Very well," Marissa agreed, passing a weary hand across her forehead.

Giving her a peck on the cheek, Marc turned to the washbasin, rolling up his sleeves and scrubbing his hands and forearms with strong soap. "What's the man's name?" he called over his shoulder to the lumberjacks clustered around the injured man.

When Marc turned to face the men, he witnessed an exchange of glances, followed by a casual shrug of burly shoulders. "We don't know," said one. "He just blew into town this afternoon on the train. We don't know who he is . . . and don't rightly care, neither!"

"Billy LeFave!" the patient bawled out unexpectedly, causing the wound to spurt a stream of bright red blood. He gritted his strong, white teeth and swallowed as if choking down a spasm of pain. "Now that you know my name . . . you'll not be forgetting Billy LeFave again!"

As the warning died away, his fingers curled toward the seeping hole in his chest, and an ominous, gurgling sound could be heard.

Marc and Marissa's gaze met as she paused in the doorway, and he approached the operating table where the lumberjacks were gathered around, holding the hapless man on the table.

"Scalpel, please, Harmony," Marc said in a weary voice, as if oblivious to the keening wail that had emanated from an upstairs bedroom where Rose Grant was closeted with Joy.

So anguished was the cry that Marissa knew instantly that while the heathen girl might not understand English, she had recognized the name "Billy LeFave," and it had struck terror to her heart. "Lord help us," she prayed as she quietly shut the door to the operating room.

Instead of going directly to the master bedroom, she climbed the stairs and went down the hall, pausing in front of a door and rapping lightly. "It's me, Rose," she whispered. "I came up to help you with Joy. . . ."

"And it's help I'm needin'," Rose said, hurrying to let her in. "I had near about calmed the girl down, and now she's in an absolute state! Whoever it is that Doc's attendin' to, his name means something to this poor child. And judgin' by her actions, it's an unpleasant and vile association."

"He's an evil man," Marissa murmured. "I can sense it . . . and I know that Marc does, too. I don't know what . . . that man . . ." she quickly censored herself before she repeated the fearful name, "means to Joy, but I know I intend to protect her from him. I'm not sure how . . . for it's clear Dr. Wellingham will have to admit the patient to the infirmary. I'm not afraid of him, nor will Harmony mind nursing him, but I don't want Joy to have to confront him again. I guess I'd feel better if he didn't even know she was here."

"She won't be for much longer," Rose declared.

Marissa looked shocked. "What do you mean? Has she tried to escape?"

"No." Rose shook her head. "I'm takin' her back to the hotel with me. We have plenty of empty rooms and I can guard her well there. She trusts me, Marissa, the way she hasn't come to trust you and Harmony. I don't think she'll give me any trouble."

"Bless you, Rose." Marissa collected Joy's soiled garments as Rose whispered to the girl, explaining enough in Chippewa for her to understand that they intended to keep her safe. "And Godspeed. . . ."

chapter
4

AFTER SEEING ROSE and the girl called Joy out the back door, Marissa turned away. She was too tired to observe the two women's progress in the glow of the coal-oil lantern that swung at Rose's side. But she knew that the bobbing rays of light would illuminate their way across the side yard and down the well-traveled path leading uptown to the mercantile and the Grant Hotel.

Marissa retrieved hot water from the reservoir of the wood range, poured it into a pitcher and ewer, retreated to the master bedroom, and quickly sponged off before she slipped into a crisp, cotton nightgown. Then she brushed her hair smooth and slid between the sheets, falling asleep almost before her head had come to rest on the plump feather pillow.

Thus occupied, she was unaware of the moans issuing from Marc's surgical quarters. Nor did she hear the pounding thuds of a logger's boots as he, unable to withstand the gory scene a moment longer, ran for the back door and hung over the railing, retching weakly.

It was after midnight before Marc ordered Harmony to get some rest. She did so only after restoring order to the operating room, discarding the blood-stained linens in a basket for the next day's wash. Marc himself took up a position in a chair near the bed to monitor the condition of Billy LeFave, who lay suspended between life and death.

Leaning forward, Marc noted that LeFave's blustery swagger had been subdued by the laudanum he had administered, as well as the severe blood loss the man had sustained from the gunshot wound to his chest. Beneath his swarthy complexion, the patient was as wan and waxen as the flame flickering near his bed.

Once asleep, Marissa didn't awaken until the grandfather clock had bonged four times. She rolled over, felt for her husband's form on the pillow beside her, and realized that he had not yet come to bed.

Rising quietly, she scuffed into her slippers. She secured her robe about her, tying her sash, then fumbled for matches and lit a miniature kerosene lamp. Inserting her finger through the glass loop, she held it up and carefully made her way through the dark house.

She found Marc in the infirmary, his head slumped forward on his chest, his face haggard with weariness. Gently she touched his arm, and he groaned softly but did not awaken.

"Marc, wake up . . . come to bed, darling," Marissa urged. "You're exhausted. You can't rest in that straight-backed chair. Come on . . . get up and let's get you to bed." She firmly nudged him awake.

"The patient—" Marc groggily protested.

"He'll be all right," Marissa whispered. "If you don't get more rest than you have these past few days, Dr. Wellingham, *you're* going to be laid out in the cot next to him!"

"He'll—"

"He won't be alone. I'll sit with Mr. LeFave, and if his condition changes, I'll rouse you immediately. I promise."

"All right." Marc rose and stretched, working the kinks from his spine.

"I'll get Harmony to help later, but unless there's a turn

for the worse, we won't summon you," Marissa said. "You've done what you could this night, Marc. The rest is up to the Lord."

Marissa left LeFave's side only long enough to see her husband to bed before she retraced her steps and positioned herself in the chair Marc had recently vacated. She adjusted the kerosene lamp on a night table beside the bed, drew the chair closer, and extracted from the drawer a Bible, placed there for patients' use during their stay in the infirmary.

Softly, Marissa read aloud, her fingers tenderly flipping page after page of the Good Book as she made her way through Proverbs, filled with poetic words of comfort and wisdom.

By the time the grandfather clock had struck six times, the first rays of morning were firing the tops of the pines. With a sigh Marissa boosted herself off the hard seat and massaged the stiffness in her back with one knuckle. Then she replaced the Bible in the drawer, snuffed out the glow of the coal-oil lamp, and padded from the room, knowing that Billy LeFave would be all right unattended for no longer than it would take her to put on water for coffee.

That chore attended to, Marissa climbed the stairs and made her way down the hall to Harmony's quarters, rapping lightly on the door. "Harmony, I'm letting Doctor sleep in this morning. He was terribly tired when I found him in the patient's room. I'd appreciate it if you could attend to the patient's needs while I make breakfast."

"Coming," Harmony said, yawning, and Marissa heard her feet hit the shiny hardwood floor. "Be right there."

Marissa returned to look in on LeFave before she went into the kitchen. She was adding a few chunks of stovewood when Harmony joined her.

To look at the pretty young woman, one wouldn't have guessed that she had been up until the wee hours, helping with surgery and nursing a critically ill patient. Her hair was neatly braided, and her gown was fresh and crisp.

"I'll help you with the laundry as soon as Dr. Wellingham is able to take over with Mr. LeFave, or deems the patient sufficiently well to be unattended for a while," Harmony offered. "Between Joy's bath, our drenching in the process, and surgery last night, the supply of fresh linens is almost depleted."

Marissa sighed wearily. "All right. But only if Marc doesn't need you." A slight pucker creased her brow. "Maybe Molly could help me today, or I could ask Rose to send one of her daughters to lend a hand for a few hours. That is, if she can spare someone, considering that she has Joy on her hands."

"Yes, and more capable hands than ours, it seems." Harmony's tone was rueful, but her blue eyes were twinkling.

"They really did seem to take to one another, didn't they?" Marissa mused as she poured them each a cup of coffee and placed hot corn muffins, butter, and maple syrup on the table between them.

"Yes, they did. At least, after Rose spoke a few words in Chippewa. It was a true blessing that she remembered enough to reassure the poor girl."

Marissa nodded. "She said she hadn't spoken the dialect in so many years that it was a miracle it came back to her at all. From what she said, it's been nearly thirty years since she was friends with a little Chippewa girl in her home back in North Dakota."

"I truly doubt we could've managed without Rose." Harmony gave a helpless laugh. "What a sight we must've made!"

Marissa chuckled along with her. "I think I was still in a state of shock when we tackled Joy's bath. I couldn't believe my eyes when I laid eyes on your 'guest'. . . and caught a good, stout whiff of her, too!"

They sipped their coffee in silence, savoring the quiet moment before Marissa spoke up again. "By the way, Harmony Childers, I think you owe me some explanations! How on earth did you happen to end up with Joy in the first place?"

Harmony sighed and shook her head in a gesture of disbelief. "To make a long and very complicated story as brief as possible . . . Lester *bought* her."

Marissa choked on her sip of coffee and her eyes widened. "What?! Lester? *Our* Lester bought *a woman?*"

Harmony nodded. "You heard me right, 'Rissa. But it's not at all like it sounds."

"But why?" Marissa whispered, stunned.

"It was a terrible accident."

Marissa shook her head, confused. "How on earth can you purchase another human being—which sounds to me like an unlawful transaction—and consider it 'an accident'?"

Harmony gave a helpless shrug. "Poor Lester didn't realize that he was bidding on a red-haired girl. In good faith Les actually believed he was bidding on a beautiful sorrel filly—a fine horse he coveted from the moment he laid eyes on her."

"Heavens!" Marissa gasped.

"It would almost be funny," Harmony ventured, "if Lester didn't view it as such a tragedy." Quickly she explained, revealing how the words the trapper had used to describe Joy also perfectly applied to the prancing red horse. "He had the winning bid—seventy-five dollars—which is a princely sum for a horse. But Les was determined to have that filly. Instead, the trapper handed over Joy."

"Lester must've been thunderstruck!"

"That's putting it mildly. He was furious! And so disappointed to learn that the beautiful filly wasn't his and that he'd taken on another human being instead and forfeited his savings in the bargain."

Marissa shook her head, dazed. "Knowing Lester, he's going to be awhile getting over this."

Harmony gave a quick nod. "Especially if the men razz him, should word get out. Why, to hear Les tell it, he became the laughingstock of all the townspeople gathered in front of the livery."

"Poor Lester!"

"The only ones who didn't mock and ridicule him without mercy were some of the Indian braves. Lester felt they were almost as uncomfortable as he, and certainly not amused at all. Seems they sympathized with Joy's plight when the trapper who sold her struck her viciously, right in front of the crowd, before he rode off, vowing never to return to the area."

"Well, good riddance to him, I'd say," Marissa sniffed.

"Very likely all of Warroad is abuzz over the goings-on," Harmony murmured. "I'm afraid it's only a matter of time before the news reaches Williams. Lester will just have to live this down."

Marissa rose to refill the coffeepot. "I'm sure he'll manage somehow. God will provide Lester the strength and humility to endure the catcalls."

"I reminded Les of that yesterday. I also informed him that the Lord doesn't make mistakes and that in his sovereignty, he must've intended for Lester to do what he did in order to serve his purpose . . . whatever that might be."

Marissa frowned in reflection. "You mean, Lester was not willing to turn to the Lord with this problem?"

Harmony nodded reluctantly. "Well, it's a powerful test of his faith, at least. Several times I had to remind him of his Christian principles, or he'd have left Joy standing in the streets of Warroad all by her lonesome."

Marissa quaked at the prospect. She'd been in the area long enough to know what some of the residents were like. It was a known fact that more than a few of the area's rougher citizens were fugitives from the law, preferring to endure the rigors of the harsh and sometimes hostile wilderness than the close confines of a prison cell. "What a cruel and debauched existence that would have been," she said, remembering her own mistakes of the past and knowing only too well how cruel the world can be to those who are cast out of their family circle.

"Joy seems afraid of Lester," Harmony said, "but I shudder to think what she'd have had to fear from some of the others who bid for her."

"Someone like Billy LeFave?"

"What?" Harmony asked, confused, as their new patient suddenly entered the breakfast conversation.

"Joy's not totally ignorant of the English language," Marissa said with a knowing look.

"Really? What do you mean?"

"The poor girl nearly went into a frenzy when Mr. LeFave began to yell out his name."

Harmony's cup clattered into her saucer, her eyes wide with alarm. "*Joy* knows *him?* Oh, dear . . . this may be worse than I thought."

"Joy's reaction was as if the Devil incarnate was in the house with her. She was terribly relieved to leave with Rose . . . and she was careful that not so much as a scrap of evidence remained behind to give away the fact that she'd ever been here."

Harmony rubbed her arms where the goosebumps peppered her flesh, followed by a prickly chill. "Then Joy's life may be in danger, for I know Billy LeFave has killed before. And I know it's wrong of me to judge . . . but I can't help thinking that, if he lives, he'll kill again."

"Harmony, how do you know? I overheard the lumberjacks say he was a stranger in town."

"The barkeep from the Black Diamond came over about midnight to learn the patient's fate, and he told us about Mr. LeFave's past," she replied. "Rather an unsavory existence to date, I'd say. And barring a miracle, I'd venture to say the future won't be any different."

"Which is?"

"Thieving. Gambling. Drinking. Squandering his time and money on bawdy women," Harmony admitted, blushing and choking over the coarse litany. "Even . . . cold-blooded *murder!*"

"No!" Marissa gasped, growing pale as she considered the man whose life her husband had labored unto exhaustion to save. "Murder . . ." Her hand, unbidden, dropped to her waist that was thickening with the bulk of her coming babe. "If that's true . . . then why is he a free man?"

"Billy LeFave killed the son of a Chippewa chief farther south of here."

Marissa exploded. "I should think with that act he signed his own death warrant!"

"My thought, exactly," Harmony agreed, "until the bar-

66

keep explained tribal customs. The Chippewa code of conduct allows for the family of the murder victim to decide the fate of the murderer. They consider it a 'right of revenge.' Relatives may avenge the death of a slain family member by killing the murderer. Or, as strange as it may seem, they can adopt the murderer into the family!"

"So Billy LeFave was one of the fortunate ones who was forgiven and adopted?"

"Yes."

Marissa sank back down into her chair, kneading her aching back. "Obviously the chief's mercy was great . . . and I'm not sure Mr. LeFave even deserved it." She was thoughtful for a long moment. "But then, in all honesty, how many of us deserve to be forgiven when the Lord redeems us and washes away our sins?"

Harmony nodded in understanding. "Mama used to talk a lot about how folks come into our lives, weaving in and out like threads in a beautiful tapestry. She said no one crosses our path but what there's a reason behind it. Just yesterday, after we 'acquired' Joy, I was reminding Les of that. There's a reason why she's in our lives. . . ." She gazed out the kitchen window. "Now I'm thinking that maybe there's a reason why Billy LeFave is in our lives—beneath our very roof. Maybe the Lord has a special purpose for him, too."

"Perhaps you're right," Marissa mused. "But from his background, I'll admit, I'm a little uneasy about finding out exactly what that purpose is."

"I felt that way, too, at first," Harmony admitted. "But then I reminded myself that no one—not Billy LeFave nor any other mortal man—could harm so much as a hair on our heads unless the Lord allowed it. And if the Lord allowed it, then it would only be in order that his greater plan be served and his glory revealed."

Marissa shook her head in amazement. "Much as I can admire the action, it's hard for me to conceive of that Indian father adopting the murderer of his beloved son. Yet it's easier to fathom that thought than to understand the love of our heavenly Father, whose mercy knows no bounds. The way I see it, if the Indian chief chose to let Billy LeFave live, and if the Lord spared him from what should have been a mortal wound, then there's a purpose behind Billy LeFave's continuing to draw breath on this earth. Maybe God intends to claim Billy as his own one day."

"I hope you're right, 'Rissa," Harmony said. "But I'll have to say that before the apothecary preparations rendered Mr. LeFave unconscious, his behavior was pureful awful! And such language! I wouldn't begin to repeat it!"

"And how many times does Holy Scripture tell us of men—and women, too—who were out-and-out rotters but were counted among the righteous when they gave their lives to Christ?"

"That's true. . . ."

"And with that thought in mind, even if Billy LeFave is motionless as a boulder when I sit with him in the sickroom, I'm going to read the Scriptures aloud to him each and every day. Marc has told me that, even when one is unconscious, it's believed they can hear. So if that's true . . . then I pray that words of wisdom from the Good Book will stick in Billy LeFave's mind and soften his hard heart so that one day he'll accept the Good News of salvation. . . ."

chapter
5

Rose Grant quietly cracked the door open and peeked into the dimly lit hotel room where she had deposited a damp and exhausted Joy the night before. She had coerced the resistant girl there with the assistance of Homer Ames, who was far more fluent in the Chippewa dialect than she. Together, they had convinced Joy that they meant her no harm and that she would be safe in their custody.

Rose started with alarm when she viewed the empty bed with its rumpled linens. Somehow, despite her best precautions, Joy had escaped!

Just as Rose was about to sound the alarm, she stepped farther into the room and spied the redheaded girl fast asleep, curled up in a ball on the braid rug that cushioned the hardwood oak floor. She pulled the heavy door to, leaving Joy to sleep on undisturbed. But her mind was spinning with the events of the past twenty-four hours.

Hearing the bell ring at the desk, Rose had entered the hotel lobby, feeling a sudden swooning sensation, as if she were drifting through a thrilling dream from which she prayed never to awaken. There, completely unexpectedly, she had come face-to-face with the man of her dreams—Homer Ames—the childhood sweetheart she had loved all her life.

Even now she had to pinch herself, coming in contact with an arm that was now slim and pretty where not so long ago wattles of dimpled flesh had hung from her frame. And she couldn't help being thankful that, due to Molly Masterson's concerns about her own weight, Rose had been persuaded to count her calories. And just in time! What if Homer had found her three times the tiny slip of a girl he remembered from long ago!

When their eyes had met, Rose's lips had parted in delighted amazement. Even though it had been many years since she had seen Homer, her heart skipped a beat, for she'd have recognized him anywhere!

For a moment she couldn't speak as she made her way around to the rear of the marble-top counter where hotel guests checked in, and her heart fluttered disturbingly. "As I live and breathe, it's Homer Ames!" Rose whispered, feeling her cheeks heat with pleasure. "At your service," he replied, smiling. "It's so good to see you, Rose, dear, and to find you looking so well. Especially since, thanks to contacts with Luke Masterson of the Meloney Lumber Company, I've learned that a number of misfortunes have befallen you and your family in recent months."

"It's a fact we've been through some hard times of late," Rose admitted. She drew in a deep breath and met Homer's steady gaze, lost in the dark depths of his eyes. "But the Lord has been faithful to provide for me and mine."

Homer gave an admiring shake of his head. "Praise God, you're the same old Rose," he said warmly, "with a shining faith as bright as your beauty that certainly hasn't dimmed through the years, I see."

Rose blushed prettily. It had been ages since anyone had spoken flirtatious words to her. Years since she had been free to listen and to treasure the sweet sentiments. "And you're the same old Homer," she countered, "full of tender words and flatterin' observations."

"No, my dear, I'm merely a man who speaks the truth as he finds it. Some things never change, Rosie . . . and one of them is my love for you."

"Oh . . . Homer!" Rose breathed, her eyes growing misty. She had longed to hear this declaration for all the years of the loveless marriage arranged by her father for profit.

Slowly, serenely, Homer opened his arms in silent invitation.

Feeling like a schoolgirl in love and scarcely aware of her surroundings, Rose followed the call of her heart. As if pulled along by a force stronger than herself, she was swept toward Homer and into his strong and sheltering embrace. And when his hands gently cupped the curve of her shoulder, she felt as if she were home—truly home—for the first time in many, many years.

A suspicious moisture tingled behind Rose's eyes. She wasn't sure if the tears were from joy . . . or regret over what she had been denied through the years.

Without warning, Homer's lips brushed Rose's smooth cheek, soft with the fresh scent of talc. "I've never forgotten you, Rose."

She lifted her face from his shoulder the fraction of an inch required to look into his eyes. "Nor I, you."

"I love you, Rosie."

She sighed with contentment, clinging to him. "Once I started lovin' you years ago, Homer, there was no stopping the feelings of my heart, even though I'd foolishly married another."

He nodded soberly and patted Rose's arm. "Uncond-itional love, Rose, once freely given, can't be purloined."

"It feels so good to be in your arms," she whispered.

"It's where I pray you'll always remain," he murmured.

"Oh . . . I'm so glad we stayed in touch all these years . . . though we did it proper-like, since I was a married woman."

Homer nodded against her soft hair. "It eased my grief a little, Rose, to know that you were alive and well . . . even if you were sharing your life with another man."

"I steeled myself to read in the newspaper one day that you'd married," Rose admitted, "knowin' I'd be apt to suffer a pang of envy if I did."

Homer chuckled, his breath caressing Rose's ear as he clasped her even tighter in an impulsive hug. "An impossibility, Rosie, for I never cared for another woman as I did for you. Rather than settle for something less, I was content to live out my days as a bachelor, hoping that if you were ever free, you'd give me a second chance at love. And if not . . . well, I knew we'd be together for all eternity with the Lord in heaven."

"Oh, Homer," she breathed, "that was *my* private hope, too. The years we've been apart haven't been easy. In fact . . ."

"Shh . . . I know," Homer soothed, smoothing her neat brunette coronet, shot through with silver strands. "We've a lot of catching up to do, Rose. But first things first. . . ." He gestured toward the hotel register. "I'd best find a room in this establishment."

Rose's cheeks flushed rosier still. "I declare I'm so thrilled to see you that my senses seem to have taken leave." She slipped out of his arms, her limbs feeling weak with ecstasy, and went through the motions of signing Homer Ames in as a guest of the Grant Hotel.

"What brings you to Williams?" Rose asked as she led the way to his suite.

"Seeing you, of course, Rose. But after I learned from Luke that you and your children were left alone this past winter, I decided to wait a decent interval before combining business with a private reunion. I wanted to give you time to recover and to adjust to your grief and loss before I appeared."

"Alas, the marriage was such that, under the circumstances, I'm afraid I was more relieved than grieved when I became a widow. My husband turned out to be a drunkard, you see, and a heathen—a faithless bloke who begrudged me my love for the Lord. We were at odds for many years . . . over just about everything."

"Perhaps the two of you were always at odds just as we—you and I—were somehow always one, even though apart, Rose."

"Yes! Yes, that's exactly how it was!" she cried softly, realizing that it had been oo.

"But we're together now. And I want us—one day soon—to be together for always."

Rose's soft, expressive eyes twinkled. "I do declare, Mr. Ames, that sounds very much like a proposal."

Homer cleared his throat, giving a self-conscious smile. "I believe it is. I hope you're not offended, my dear Rose, by the suddenness of my declaration, considering . . ."

"Offended, no. Honored, yes!" Rose's reply was enthusiastic.

Homer grinned with relief. "Would you prefer I propose on bended knee, my dear?"

His lighthearted remark was teasing. But Rose sensed that Homer wanted things to be as romantic as she. "I believe I do!" she whispered, stifling a giggle.

For a fleeting moment Rose felt a bit silly when the middle-aged man dropped to one knee, tenderly took her hand in his, and asked the one question she'd never dared believe she'd hear. But there was no stemming the tears when the poignant plea—that Rose be his cherished bride—lingered in the stillness.

"Oh yes, Homer! Yes, yes, *yes!*"

"Rosie, you've just made me the happiest man in the northland," Homer whispered as he took her in his arms and pressed a tender kiss on her waiting lips. "Perhaps, years ago, I courted too slow and lost you to another. It won't happen again."

Rose shivered within his embrace. "He claimed my hand, Homer, but he never won my heart, for that has always belonged only to you."

For a long moment the two embraced, and Rose realized that Homer was a man she could depend upon, a vital part of herself that somehow made her more whole than she could be alone.

Reluctantly she moved out of his arms once more. "Supper is served in three hours," she said as she prepared to take her leave and allow Homer time to get settled into his suite. She patted at wisps of hair that curled around her cheeks, then examined the watch brooch pinned at her shoulder. "I should have a bit of time between now and then, though. I'll be down in the kitchen if you'd care to join me for coffee and talk over old times."

"And our *future*," Homer added.

"I'll be all ears!" Rose assured him with a dazzling smile, feeling dizzy at the idea of what this man's sudden appearance in her life would mean for her, for her family, for the entire town.

Making a detour to her own suite, Rose changed into a fresh frock, neatly recoiled her hair, and dabbed on a bit of lemon verbena cologne before she checked her reflection in the mirror. Even to her eyes, she looked almost as young and pretty as she had all those years ago. Or was it that they saw each other through eyes of love, blinded to the changes that time apart had wrought now that they were together again?

She was about to close the door behind her when the wink of the gold band on her left hand, reflected in the mirror on the chifferobe door, caught her attention. Rose paused only a moment, then, moving almost impulsively but with a surety about her gesture, she slid off the ring that had never left her finger. She placed it in a small silver jewel box for safekeeping. She had fulfilled her vows, had remained with her husband— beast that he was—until death parted them.

"You're free," she whispered to her reflection. "At last you're free to love again." Quick tears of joy sprang to her eyes.

Rose had scarcely had time to put on a fresh pot of coffee and place a selection of cookies on a plate when Homer joined her in the kitchen. "How like old times, Rose," he said, pausing on the threshold. "Some of the happiest hours of my life were spent with you in your ma's kitchen."

"Have a seat, have a seat," Rose said, her tone warmly brusque now that she was free to fuss and cluck over Homer the way she'd always wanted to.

She poured them both coffee and edged the plate of sugar cookies, gingersnaps, and date bars toward him. Suddenly she felt tongue-tied and nervous. Apparently so did he, for the silence lengthened between them.

"Heavens, but it's good to—" Rose began.

"I can hardly believe—" Homer started to say at exactly the same moment.

They laughed, feeling the release of tension.

Homer gazed at her across the oak table. "You're a sight most soothing to the eyes, Rose." His hand inched forward encompassing hers. With his forefinger, he caressed the ring finger of her left hand that still bore an indentation from the wedding band so recently discarded.

"And I feel as if I could happily look upon your dear features forever and forever," she murmured.

"Pray that it will be so, my love."

For a moment the two sat in silence, finding more closeness and intimacy in quietly holding hands than Rose had known in her many years of marriage.

"So tell me, Homer, how long will you be in our fair town?"

"Not as long as I would like, my dear," he admitted. "But I vow to remain for as long as it takes to make the necessary arrangements for our marriage."

"There are so many things to ponder," Rose mused.

"Guided by our hearts, the Lord will give us the right answers just when we need them."

The afternoon hours seemed to fly by as they talked of old times, sometimes laughing until the tears came.

Hearing the merriment, Rose's children came into the kitchen. One by one, they were introduced to Homer, and Rose was proud to see the approval in his eyes. But her joy was almost like a sweet pain in her breast when she saw that her children quite naturally took to Homer Ames, too, sensing that anyone so important to their ma must be important to them as well.

"We'll talk later," Rose promised Homer as she got to her feet, and she relished the fact that already she dared to lay her hand in a possessive pat on his well-groomed shoulder.

At the time Homer and Rose had made plans to discuss their future, Rose had no idea that this discussion would be postponed until so much later than she'd ever imagined. No clue that with the dawning of a new day, her life with Homer would still be unresolved.

The evening before, after hastily placing a meal before Lester Childers, she had rushed off to pick up the fabric for her wedding gown from Harmony. Now, in retrospect, she realized that Lester had been unusually pale and quiet. She had understood why only after arriving at the Wellingham home. Thinking of that chaotic scene, the events of the evening played out in her mind like some bad dream.

In only a few short hours, everything had changed. She and Homer couldn't possibly get married now! Upstairs, Joy was sleeping. And in her heart, Rose knew that she and the man she loved would have to devote themselves to settling the girl's future before they were free to plan for a lifetime together.

"Oh, Homer . . . Homer," Rose whispered as she looked around the hotel she suddenly felt owned *her*, "whatever are we goin' to do? Suddenly life is pure confusin' again."

As if echoing from a museum of memories, Rose could hear Homer's murmured admonitions from the afternoon before. And she knew that he was right.

The choices and decisions weren't entirely hers nor Homer's to make, for the Lord had a plan for them. She was confident of that. But it would be up to them to find it. . . .

chapter

6

A SOFT CLICK disturbed the early-morning stillness of the
room on the third floor of the Grant Hotel. Min-O-Ta, the
surly redhead called "Good Heart" by her adopted people,
stirred at the subtle sound that had penetrated her consciousness as she lay on the hardwood floor in a state somewhere
between deep sleep and full awakening.

Her eyes flicked open. She stared at the whitewashed ceil-
ing overhead and then at the curly cloth that tickled her nose
and cheek as she lay curled in a ball beside the strange sleeping platform where the pleasant-faced woman had insisted
she stretch out the night before. Then, Min-O-Ta had been
too exhausted to protest, so she had obliged, allowing herself
to sink into a stuporous sleep, sensing that the older squaw
meant her no harm.

Harm!

Min-O-Ta's fingers, which still felt tender at the very tips
where the yellow-haired woman with the rounding belly had
dug beneath her dirty nails with a metal stick, flew to her
neck. Her magic charm was gone!

Min-O-Ta resisted the urge to scream and, like a good
Chippewa, held her peace stoically. Even in her anguish, she
made no noise.

As a child, she had learned that it was necessary for the
well-being of the tribe for children to remain quiet. Infants
were not allowed to squall, for a wailing child could give away

the location of their camp to nearby enemies. Even a muffled outcry could bring down dire consequences on their tribe. Min-O-Ta had learned long ago to bridle her tongue, though she sometimes felt as if she might burst with the effort.

Even so, in the face of what might be in store for her, the girl could not restrain a feathery moan that she hoped carried no farther than the closed doors.

Gingerly she sat up, her fingertips still at her neck, searching for the good medicine that had hung on a rawhide thong around her neck. It was a talisman given to her by the tribe's shaman, an ancient old hag who had put it there, promising that it would keep her safe from evil spirits and wickedness as long as she was wearing it. The old woman told Min-O-Ta that she herself had chanted incantations over the fetish that guaranteed protective powers for the wearer.

It had not occurred to Min-O-Ta that the scrap of leather containing herbs and other mysterious contents had not kept her safe from Jake's occasional brutality. But for the past several years, she had lost her fear of him, for Jake was the nearest thing to family she had left.

Born after her mother had been captured by Indians and transported to the northland where she eventually settled with a band of Chippewa Indians, Min-O-Ta had been treated as one of the tribe even though her skin was pale and her hair a flaming red. The children played together in groups, turning to whatever squaw was handy when they were hurt or in need of help. So Min-O-Ta had bonded with many women in the tribe, but most firmly with the elderly tribal shaman to whom she'd been drawn increasingly as childhood was left behind and she matured into a coltish girl.

As the years passed, Min-O-Ta's ties to her mother had grown ever fainter, and her feelings for the sons and daughters born to Sho-Busk were no deeper than what she felt for other youngsters in the tribe.

Still, it had been a rude shock to her when a big man called Jake was brought into the encampment. The chief had received him warmly, and in gratitude for saving his son from some encounter with certain death, had offered Jake anything he wanted.

Jake had chosen Sho-Busk, Min-O-Ta's mother. She was still a pretty woman then, and he was taken with her beauty and charm. Min-O-Ta was not concerned when the fierce trapper claimed Sho-Busk, but her heart had thudded in alarm when, looking about the enclosure, he had pointed out the trembling girl. He would add Min-O-Ta to his bounty!

As the three were leaving the Chippewa encampment, Sho-Busk's youngest son—a mere toddler when his father, one of the tribe's braves, killed in battle many moons before—had broken away from his playmates and pursued his mother. Jake, perhaps feeling pity for the youngster, had nodded at the chief. He would take the boy, too.

They had only traveled until nightfall before Jake was piqued to anger and offered the opinion that the recalcitrant Sho-Busk had been well named by her people. She had the attitude of a wild goat! Still, she was comely enough to please him, even if she had a mulish mind-set and as sharp a tongue as any woman he had ever met!

As days passed the newly formed unit functioned like a family. Sho-Busk, even if unwillingly, made Jake's travels easier in many ways. Min-O-Ta, fearful of having his fury directed toward herself, did as she was told.

Dressed in unrevealing buckskins, Min-O-Ta realized that Jake viewed her more as an able-bodied youth than a girl, and for that she was grateful, especially after her mother's death.

While Jake expected Min-O-Ta to take up the chores her mother had performed, he did not insist that she perform the wifely duties as well.

Min-O-Ta had not been present the day her mother and half-brother were drowned, so she could not prove her suspicions. But as she kept her ears and eyes open, trailing Jake in his travels and hauling his heavy burdens, another load was added to the invisible weight her heart had always borne. She was convinced that Jake had let her mother and half-brother die!

When Sho-Busk and Wa-Wa-Tay's sled had crashed through a patch of rotten ice, plummeting into the icy depths, Jake had made no effort to fish the struggling woman and her son from the frigid water. Instead, he had focused on snatching back the sled and sodden fur bundles before they could sink from sight, robbing him of the profits already gathered during the winter months.

And although Min-O-Ta had not been especially close to her mother and half-brother, her heart had acquired yet another layer of hardness toward Jake. She knew he was not to be trusted and that he was a man without mercy. After that, Min-O-Ta clung more fiercely than ever to the protective talisman that O-Na-Bush-O-We, the elderly shaman, had given her.

But she was not afraid of Jake. Having decided that he was only superior to her in brute strength, Min-O-Ta feared him only when he was unhappy with her or had been drinking firewater and considered it his due to strike her and cuff her until her vision blurred and her headaches returned.

Even so, considering how some slaves in the tribe had been treated—whether captives from other Indian tribes or white victims of kidnapping—Min-O-Ta was aware that her lot was better than most. For Jake, viewing her as a possession of some value, had not overly mistreated her, knowing that scars and bruises would erode her worth in the marketplace.

He had concocted a scheme that continued to work, time after time. Setting up camp at a likely location, he would gather a group of men and offer Min-O-Ta for sale on the slave block . . . though he had no intention of making good the deal. After the transaction was made and the money was safely in his pocket, Jake would give her detailed instructions for slipping away from her new "owner" in order to rendezvous somewhere down the trail before traveling on to their next destination.

Still, he fed her well and allowed her sufficient time to rest to keep her body strong and her complexion glowing. And since she had often seen Jake bested in fights with other men, she gained a certain perverse satisfaction in her favored estate, believing that the talisman had worked strong magic against him.

Until yesterday. . . .

For the first time in many moons, Jake had struck fear into her heart with his vile epithets, raining down curses on her, spelling out the consequences if she defied him or tried to thwart his plans. In a loud bellow, Jake had rattled off the names of evil spirits and demons, those O-Na-Bush-O-We had only dared whisper, lest they overhear and seek vengeance. He had warned Min-O-Ta that she must be obedient to her new master or the evil spirits would mete out fearful retribution.

It was at that moment that she realized he truly intended to abandon her to another. Her heart had quailed at the prospect.

For as fearsome as Jake could be, especially when he was raging from the effects of firewater, he was infinitely less threatening than the quiet man with the simmering eyes and the flinty face into whose custody she had been remanded.

When the auction had begun, Min-O-Ta had not believed that Jake would really sell her. Before, he had only gone through the motions. And a time or two, she had been only briefly in another master's company before managing to slip away and rejoin Jake.

But this time, he had given her no such orders. He had been drinking firewater, and when he did, he tended to forget things. Now she realized it had not been an oversight at all.

Never before had he called down evil spirits upon her. And never before had he ridden away, calling out that he'd not be back!

After Jake had disappeared, Min-O-Ta observed the young man to whom she'd been sold. He was tall—taller than she—but not as big and burly as Jake. The fleeting thought flitted through Min-O-Ta's mind that in a fight, she might even be able to best him. After all, she'd learned some of her dirtiest, most ruthless methods of protecting herself from Jake!

In studying the fellow, she concluded that he was pleasant to look upon—a great improvement over Jake. But that's where her relief ended. Jake had grown lax toward Min-O-Ta, giving her some moments for which she did not have to account. But her new owner seemed anything but pleased about having her in his company. That made no sense. For if he disliked her so much, then why had he parted with his cash so eagerly?

The man had appeared to stand rooted to the earth, grounded in indecision, so Min-O-Ta had stood quietly near-by, patiently waiting for a clue as to what would come next.

Nothing.

The others had wandered away and she and the lean man

were still standing as statues when they were approached by a young woman with hair the color of honey in the bee tree. The man seemed to know her.

This sweet-faced, yellow-haired one looked as friendly and pleasant as the man appeared fierce and scowling. Min-O-Ta had listened to their heated exchange. She'd had no idea what they were saying, but from the man's gestures, she concluded that it involved her. And that, just as she had suspected, he was not pleased with his bargain.

Min-O-Ta had felt relief when he'd stomped away. But then the pretty woman had spoken to him, causing him to stop in his tracks and face them. Then with obvious reluctance, he had done the golden-haired woman's bidding.

Feeling confusion unlike anything she'd known in her many seasons, Min-O-Ta had stood motionless until the woman had made clear to her that she was expected to go with them. She had obeyed, only because rebellion would release all the forces of evil against her. With that thought in mind, she had crept close to them, dogging their tracks. Min-O-Ta was wearier than she had ever been as they trooped here and there and finally boarded the noisy, huffing contraption she had only seen from a distance. When the woman offered her food to eat, Min-O-Ta realized how hungry she was. She couldn't recall just when she'd last eaten, for when Jake was in the white man's town, he had preferred to drink, giving little thought to nourishment.

Realizing that this food might constitute her last meal, Min-O-Ta had eaten quickly so that none would go to waste. It was gone before she knew it, leaving her hungering for more.

Almost as if he could read her mind—which frightened Min-O-Ta—the man had offered her his food. Her fear was underscored as she imagined the kinds of evils that could beset her if this man was able to know her most private thoughts. Jake had never had such powers. It was good, for some of her thoughts toward him would have earned her the back of his hand across her face. Or worse.

All these puzzling thoughts had filled her mind the evening before when they had brought her to this large structure, so different from the bark huts and tepees of her people. The yellow-haired one and another woman with a rounded belly had almost scalded her in a kettle of water, trying to drown her, and then had scoured at her skin as if attempting to strip her hide. Then another had come, a woman whose name sounded like that of a flower, and had spoken to her in Chippewa.

It was this woman who had brought her to another, even larger tepee. Inside, up some steps, she had been brought to this place where the woman had turned down blankets, much like Min-O-Ta's mother had turned down pelts, and gestured to her, bidding her to climb into the surprisingly soft platform.

Splaying her fingers across Min-O-Ta's forehead, the woman with the name of a flower had gently forced her back against a fluffy cushion, wordlessly conveying that she should remain there and rest. As tired as Min-O-Ta felt and the way her head had ached, unrelieved by the blue dot that the tribe's medicine man had tattooed on her temple to ward off the pain in her skull, it had felt good to close her eyes and surrender to the tug of weariness.

Throughout these experiences, she had clutched the buckskin thong around her neck, her fingers in a numbing grip, as she struggled to hold fast to all that she believed stood as protection between herself and Jake's evil invections. With the charm tight in her fist, she felt safe.

Through slitted lids, Min-O-Ta had peered at the older woman, who never left her side, not even after she blew out the flame of fire that had dimly illuminated the room, glaring from a glass vessel. With no hope of escape—at least, not yet—Min-O-Ta gave in to the temptation to rest on the strange, soft platform. After all, it would help her gather her strength so as to fight her way out of the dwelling when the woman dropped her guard or fell asleep.

Following the brisk walk from the house where the women had tried to drown her, Min-O-Ta had been forced into a long and baggy garment. It reminded her of a gunnysack such as Jake had used to bundle his possessions together for transport. Dispirited, the girl considered how hampering such a flimsy, loose garment would be compared to her buckskins that were warm, durable, and protected her from briars, thorns, and stinging insects. She would have to somehow find her moccasins, too, she realized, for the strange and unbearably stiff foot coverings that the yellow-haired woman and the others had forced on her feet, hobbled her gait like a tethered pony.

Such swirling considerations made Min-O-Ta feel as if she were sinking into a warm, deep black lake. She vowed that she would only float there for a moment, using the time to rest and to plot her escape.

But Min-O-Ta hadn't meant to sleep so long. Nor had she been aware of leaving the platform to seek the hard level ground.

The woman, Rose, was no longer standing guard.

But neither was Min-O-Ta's cherished talisman.

Terror ricocheted through her slender frame. The white

woman—the kind one with the name of a flower—knew the Chippewa language. Perhaps she also knew that the talisman was strong medicine, and coveted it for her own! Perhaps she had stolen it for her own protection! She must get it back, Min-O-Ta decided, just as she had to find a way to reclaim her buckskins. And her moccasins.

Min-O-Ta's stomach growled hungrily. Her head throbbed. Her mouth felt dry, her tongue swollen. She wished for nothing more than to be able to hunker on the sand beside the lake and bring water to her lips in a cupped hand, or to lie on the bank overhanging a small creek and slake her thirst.

In these strange surroundings, Min-O-Ta had no idea what to do. She only knew that she must leave this place, must somehow retrace the maze of steps, bringing her back to the sheltering haven of the forest where she would once again feel at home.

But when Min-O-Ta recalled the only words she had recognized the night before—*Billy LeFave*—she trembled with fear. She was alone now, and unprotected by Jake or her talisman. She dared not venture from this place, for when she considered the possibility of encountering him again, the prospect of remaining in the company of the Rose woman was infinitely less frightening!

chapter
7

LESTER FACED THE morning with a heart that felt as empty as his pockets. So he was downcast, his face drawn as he appeared at the Meloney Brothers Lumber Company offices to accept his assignment for the day.

He'd counted on having one of the Meloney mounts available to him, but it was not to be. The fact that he was consigned to be afoot while making his rounds instead of sitting proudly astride the sorrel horse of his dreams only served to deepen his sense of despair.

Lester grimly accepted a ride on a swing-dingle en route to one of the camps. At least it would take him partway to the timberland he was to look over for possible acquisition by the company. Afterward Lester planned to walk to the nearest lumber camp to seek lodging for the night before hitching a ride back to Williams in a day or two. There would surely be a teamster taking a wagon to town or maybe he could prevail upon a company official with a carriage to help him out. In any case, he didn't intend to make use of shank's mare on the return trip, if he could help it.

As was their custom, lumbermen on the swing-dingle joked with Lester, then looked puzzled when he failed to respond in his usual jovial manner. He could sense their questioning glances, the stealthy nudges, the lifted brows as they made silent inquiry. But the only answer forthcoming was the shake of a head or a mystified shrug.

At the designated site, Lester hopped down from the swing-dingle to set out on foot. He managed what he hoped passed for a cheery wave and headed into the thick timber as the company employees continued on their way.

Pausing for a moment to get his bearings, he proceeded due east and clambered over a deadfall, a thatch of fallen trees and branches. His assignment for the day was to scout out a piece of promising land for lease or purchase. If he found a likely spot, he would then recommend that the company acquire rights to move in and harvest the timber.

Les had already learned one lesson well: Here in the north woods, while he could let down his guard in some ways, he had to keep doubly alert in others. For example, in this area where the climate was considered almost arctic compared to the balmier central Illinois region, there were no poisonous snakes. Only rarely had Lester come across even a common garter snake. He found it rather pleasant not to have to carefully examine the spot where he was about to plant his foot so as not to step on a venomous timber rattler, water moccasin, or copperhead.

Nevertheless, he had to keep an eye out for bears and wolves that traveled in packs and could ring a lone man and move in for the kill before he knew it. He was grateful that Luke, recognizing the inherent dangers, had furnished him a pistol. For Lester took seriously the everyday dangers that some lumberjacks scoffed at to impress their peers with their derring-do.

The day was balmy and the woods pleasantly serene as Lester penetrated ever deeper. The sighing of the wind through the pine boughs was all that broke the stillness, except for the occasional protest of a bluejay, the cry of a loon, or the snapping of brush that startled a herd of white-tailed deer grazing in a small clearing. With a graceful leap, they bounded off in alarm.

For a few more minutes, Lester basked in the sunshine filtering through the thick trees and breathed deeply of the pine-scented air.

As a man who'd grown up in the midst of timberlands, he had an appreciation for the fine stands of virgin pine that could be felled to create lovely homes and generate impressive profits for the company. In his pocket he carried a folded scrap of parchment and a stub of a lead pencil, ready to make notations of the size, quality, and quantity of harvestable lumber available. Occasionally he unsheathed his hatchet and notched some of the trees, etching signs in the rough bark that would identify prime timber should the deal go through.

Moving purposefully now, he remained on guard as he climbed over tangled masses of vines and low-growing brush, thrashed his way through bramble patches that tore at his clothing and skin, and pressed on in the general direction of the lumber camp, still several miles away.

Since arriving in Minnesota some months before, more often than he cared to remember, Lester had been reminded of the carnage that could be wrought at a lumber camp or cutting site when in one careless moment a man's life could be forever altered. He had been but a child, the eldest of the Childers young'uns, when his pa, Harmon Childers, had walked to the woods one day—healthy, happy, ambitious, and with the prospect of a bright future with his wife and their growing brood of children.

A few hours later Harm had been carried from the woods, his body crushed and broken, spilling his life blood on the golden autumn leaves that carpeted the forest floor. And before Ma, Granny Fanchon, and Grandpappy Will could get him to the doctor, the wagon jolting mercilessly over the rutted road, death had claimed him.

Even now, many years later, it seemed incredible to Lester that he and his brothers, Maylon and Thad, had eaten fried mush and hash browns with their pa at breakfast that morning and had gone off to school, fully expecting to help their pa with evening chores upon their return.

Instead, they had never seen their pa alive again. And Lester missed him. How many times had he longed to hear his pa's comforting voice or feel his affectionate touch just once more. It eased Lester's heart, though, to know that someday he would be with his father again, this time for all eternity.

For many folks, Lester knew, lumbering had been a way to make a living. And for some, it had meant the way in which they met up with death.

Harmon Childers had died in the woods. Rory Preston, his brother-in-law, who had been injured in the same grisly accident, had lived, minus a leg from the knee down.

Harm had lost his life. Rory had lost heart and faith.

Harm had died quickly. Rory had been stricken with a lingering wasting away that had slowly drained his spirit.

The entire community, along with Rory's blood kin, had watched him turn from the faith of his fathers and blaspheme the God he'd always believed was loving and trustworthy. But in his hurt, Rory had come to view him as an adversary, an enemy not to be trusted, a meddling punisher, a consummate practical joker who pleasured in thwarting a man's plans and savoring their foibles and frustrations.

It was difficult to reconcile that wild and faithless man, though, with the transformed Rory who had returned to the area with a new wife and a strong, revitalized faith. He was now a loving family man with a conviction as stout as that of his big sister, Lizzie, whose beliefs had never wavered through all the tragedies of her own life.

Lester knew his ma had given thanks many times that Rory had found Sylvia Hyatt, a godly woman who had appealed to her brother as no one ever had. It was nothing short of a miracle, she'd said. Even Lester had heard the whisperings among the good people of Salt Creek. Rumor had it that his uncle had socialized with some unsavory types, and Lester realized how easily he could have chosen another kind of woman to share his life.

For a moment, Lester thought of his own pathway. With a helpless shiver that peppered his flesh with goosebumps, he realized that he had not yet known such moments of trial and testing as had the others—Uncle Rory . . . Alton . . . Brad . . . his mother, Lizzie. So far, life had not asked of him more than he was willing to give.

Oh, it had been extremely hard on the Childers family when Pa died, of course. But Ma had kept the family going, with a faith that was as flinty and firm as ever.

And the Lord had been good to provide Jeremiah Stone to step in and lend a hand in Harm's place. Jem, a family friend, had been there to help Lester and his brothers learn what they would need to know to take their places in the world. And he had been there to supply Lizzie with all the love and romance she had lost.

Then when Jeremiah had gone on to his reward, his ma had found another love. Brad Mathews had appeared to ease her aching heart and fill her arms with his own motherless children. Ma had said it was no accident. That the Good Lord, knowing he would call Harm and Jem home early, had planned from the beginning to bring Brad and Lizzie together to live out their days.

Ma had faith, all right. Her convictions were soft as goosedown when sympathy and solace were needed but tough as rawhide when she met up with evil. At those times Lizzie saw it as her Christian duty to admonish an erring believer, with liberal applications of Scripture.

Lester's fond smile faded when he recalled yet another death that was the indirect result of the lumber industry. Not many months after Grandpappy Will's death to the infirmities of old age, Granny Fanchon Preston had been battered to death in a freak buzz-saw accident when she'd sought to save a neighborhood tot from certain death. And then Jeremiah had been kicked by a maverick mule that robbed him of his senses and left him more child than man. The woodlands had claimed Miss Abby, too, when stricken with dementia, she'd wandered away and been lost in the tall trees, exposed to the elements.

But lumber- and forest-related deaths were not peculiar to Illinois, Lester knew. For just after coming to Minnesota, while serving as an apprentice to Luke Masterson, Lester had witnessed, firsthand, one of the most bizarre accidents of all.

The smithies who worked for the Meloney Brothers Lumber Company kept the massive draft horses shod with wickedly designed shoes to give them greater traction when hauling logs over the frozen ground to the sawmill. The heavy iron horseshoes were conventional in shape to fit the hooves, but there the resemblance ended. Attached to the bottom of the weighty U-shaped iron shoes were pointed steel blades forged to bite into the ice and frozen sod like teeth. Beneath the horses' weight the steel tines grew even sharper from relentless contact against snow, gravel, rock, and sand.

One particularly bitter winter afternoon, Lester had been scouting for the lumber company in an area outside of Roosevelt, a town due west of Williams, when a commotion summoned him from his work. Running to investigate, Lester saw a teamster driving a team of Percherons over the railroad crossing. Apparently, one of the horse's hooves had snagged a rail and had slid sideways for some distance down the track. As the beast struggled to right himself, the sharp tines of the shoe acted as a groove until, between one heartbeat and the next, the Percheron's hoof was securely wedged between the unyielding steel rail and the solid wooden ties of the railbed.

The horse shied and probably would have snapped its leg had the bones not been so solid. The more the horse struggled to extricate himself, the more tightly jammed the hoof and shoe became.

Far off to the east, a CNR train sounded its horn at the crossroad. Time was running out, Lester had realized with a sinking heart. Someone ought to sprint up the tracks and flag down the engineer before there was a terrible accident.

But knowing horses as he did, Lester had felt he could be of more help trying to calm the terrified animal. So he'd hurried to offer his services. And by the time he'd reached the tracks, the teamster, who was working on the horse's hind leg, was more than glad to have Lester on the other end, hanging on to the bridle to prevent the horse wedging yet another limb.

Holding him fast, Lester spoke softly, patting the horse's great neck, the tendons standing out with the effort of his struggle. The Percheron's eyes rolled wildly, and he lashed his head back and forth in a frenzy of fright, neighing pitifully. It was clear that the scream of the approaching train was as unnerving to him as it was to the men who grimly raced against the clock to free him from his predicament.

The teamster looked up from his position at the horse's hindquarters, his countenance stricken with the animal's suffering. Lester understood perfectly, for he knew how deeply a man could bond with his horse.

Although it was bitterly cold, sweat had rolled down the teamster's bearded face as his heavy mackinaw strained across his shoulders and his rugged black felt boots pounded the fresh snow to icy slickness beneath his feet.

By this time, a small crowd of curious townspeople had gathered. One raced up the track to signal the engineer. Another offered suggestions to the teamster. And someone else said he was going to hie himself off to find a sledgehammer.

Long minutes passed.

The train chugged ever closer, bellowing its warning. Looking up to see the approaching engine, the volunteer took off across the railbed, slipping, sliding, waving his blue wool stocking cap in a desperate bid to draw the engineer's attention.

The poor horse was wheezing and grunting as the teamster and several others pushed against its leg and flank, and Lester held on for dear life. Each time they made a little progress, the horse lost his balance, swayed awkwardly, and clumsily repositioned the unfettered limbs, unintentionally countering the men's best efforts to free the pinioned hoof.

A groan of despair went up and one rugged bear of a man spat in disgust, staining a nearby snowdrift with a brown stream of tobacco juice.

The iron monster hove into sight as it rounded a bend. At

that moment the winded man arrived with a sledgehammer, and there was renewed activity.

The teamster, his huge hands linked in what seemed a super-human grip, clenched the horse's hoof and pulled even as the mighty beast strained instinctively to ease the painful tension on its limb. The sledge-wielding man gave a solid tap of the hammer head against the steel shoe, then another. With a metallic clink, the hoof was forced back along the path it had taken and suddenly the Percheron's trapped leg popped free.

A cheer went up from the crowd.

The teamster let out a grunt of relief, and the man wielding the sledge cast it aside. But instead of sinking harmlessly into the snow beside the tracks, the hammer skimmed across the icy rail and struck the recently trapped animal on the fetlock. Startled, the horse kicked out in pain.

Almost simultaneously with the joyful sound of success came agonized groans of horror.

The bearded young teamster, hunkered beside the tracks, had not yet had time to arise from his cramped position behind the massive Percheron's left hind leg. As the animal kicked with lightning speed, the steel-tined back hoof, driven by the powerful muscles of his leg, slammed into the teamster's face. And the jagged iron spikes penetrated the man's skull from chin to crown.

If Lester lived to be a hundred, he'd never forget what he had seen in the horror of that moment. The gaping hole where teeth had been, rendered by the steel spike. The blood running red onto the teamster's black bushy beard as he slumped to the ground, twitching, his hands clawing for the empty eye socket. The oozing crater in the center of his forehead where his cranium had been cracked like an eggshell beneath the spike's slamming force.

Within a minute or two, the writhing woodsman lay dead. Another victim of the wilderness.

In the few months that he and Harmony had been in Minnesota, Lester had regularly downplayed his sister's concern for his safety as an employee of the lumber company. He'd teasingly called her a "worrywart." At times, annoyed, he'd even accused her of being a harpy.

But now, with the memory of that grisly death fresh in his memory, Lester found himself feeling a prickle of fear. And this time, when he thought of Harmony's admonitions, he was moved to do something about it.

Poor little Sis. Ever since she was a babe in arms, it seemed that death and dismemberment had been a part of her world. For while Pa had been killed before she was born, she had been privy to other tragedies in the family. Maybe that's why she'd taken to nursing, as a duck to water, Lester mused. Maybe she was waging a private war against old adversaries.

Nursing was a fine occupation, he thought, one for which Harmony was well-suited. The notion filled him with brotherly pride.

But suddenly another sobering thought occurred to Lester. He'd never really examined life for himself, toted up his own skills and desires, looked for a lifetime calling. He'd merely fallen into the thing that was handiest and most familiar. Lumbering and logging were all Lester Childers had known.

There had been years of various jobs in the timberlands. From the time he was a tadpole, he had helped cut firewood and had gathered kindling to keep their cabin warm. Then, as he grew taller and stronger, he'd helped his ma and pa clear the saplings, brush, and brambles away to improve the pas-turelands for their livestock.

Much later, he'd done his share of the labor required to help log the timber to build cabins and dogtrots for folks in the community. So, when Uncle Rory had come back from the Pacific Northwest a wealthy lumberman and had opened his logging enterprise with Seth Wyatt, it had seemed only natural to hire on.

Now, as Lester tramped the northern Minnesota woods, he realized that he'd fallen into his life's work almost by happen-stance. He'd never given a thought to what he would like to do, what he was best suited for. Harmony had maintained that he should have been a man of the cloth. But he'd never felt a real calling to the ministry.

Then again, he'd never felt a real calling toward anything. Not even the lumbering business in which he found himself.

Suddenly Lester felt a restlessness he'd never known before, almost painful in its intensity. Here he was, over the age of majority, and he'd lived all his life as if by rote. The fact of the matter was that while he'd been busy making a living, he'd never really lived!

He'd always done what was expected of him, had per-formed without questions the tasks laid out for him. But what if he had never fulfilled the reason for which he had been born? What if the Lord had been opening doors all along, but he'd been too blind to see them?

And there was more. The older he became, the more Lester found himself declaring that he didn't mind his bache-lor state, that he was content with his solitary existence.

But sometimes, in the dark of the night, lying in his lonely bed, Lester wondered what it would be like to love and be loved by someone special. To belong to another. To have a woman give herself to him and only to him. To be swept along on a tide of powerful emotions between a man and woman, sanctioned by the Lord who gives the gift of love to his children.

Lester found himself helpless to entertain these unbidden ideas even though old pains from the past had once convinced him never again to leave his heart unguarded. So he had put aside all thoughts of Marissa Wheeler. Still, even now, years later, Lester still vividly recalled the firestorm of conflicting emotions that had ripped through him at the news that she had run away! In leaving, Marissa had taken his heart with her, leaving him feeling helpless, alone, abandoned, seven kinds of a fool . . . and something deep within had withered and died.

Since then, there had been no desire to look at another girl. And, indeed, compared to Marissa—beautiful, intelligent, feisty—any other, no matter how lovely, would have seemed sadly wanting.

Now Lester understood that it had not been true love he'd felt for Marissa, but the fanciful dreams of a callow youth intrigued by the coltish charms of the local beauty. The two of them were as different as night and day. And if they'd married, no doubt her fiery spirit would have come to rankle him, and she'd have interpreted his quiet air of responsibility as boring, with no spunk or daring whatsoever!

Besides, Lester had liked Marc instantly and could clearly see that they were like two halves to a whole. Both Marc and Marissa made the other complete.

"Oh, that Lester, he's in love with his horses . . ." was the way most folks dismissed his bachelorhood. "But don't worry none. One of these days, some pretty little filly will catch his eye and he'll marry up just like everyone else."

They were right on one count. He'd saved his admiring glances for good horseflesh. And why not? At least he knew how to handle himself around horses. But womenfolk were another matter altogether. Especially female-types who appeared to be one way and then proved to be entirely different.

At that moment of realization, Lester had felt a strange twinge. But at the time he hadn't known what it was. Now, he knew, and he swallowed hard at the knowledge. It was a pang of envy!

Instinctively, with innocent unawareness, Lester knew that he'd actually wanted what he'd seen all around him. Something intangible he hadn't even been able to name. Now he realized that he coveted their loving relationships, even as he steadfastly maintained his decision to remain a bachelor.

Only Harmony, on the surface at least, seemed as contentedly single as he. And even she was being a bit of a pest with her matchmaking notions, proof that she was romantic Lizzie Preston Childers Stone Mathews' daughter, sure enough!

While it was flattering to know that the giggling young girls found him attractive, he couldn't think of a one of them who appealed to him enough to bother to call on her. Maybe when he found the right woman, the one intended for him by the Good Lord, he'd simply know. Time would tell. . . .

Hours later, physically and mentally tired from his day's labors and his internal wranglings, Lester neared the lumber camp where he would find a bunk and a hot meal. As he strolled into the camp, he reached for a limb and tripped, falling heavily as an unnoticed root snaked around his ankle and threw him awkwardly to the ground.

Lumberjacks turned to laugh, and Lester's cheeks flamed scarlet. How could they know—for somehow he could discern that they had heard—what had happened in Warroad only the day before?

Suddenly he wondered how he would be able to live down the debacle, wasn't sure he could risk staying in the camp through the night to be nettled unmercifully by bored workmen who had nothing better to do than to occupy themselves with his private miseries.

Once Lester had filled his belly on the cook's hearty stew, he would weigh a decision to move on. It seemed a better choice to take his chances in the deep woods than to subject himself to the speculation of those who too frequently considered love a staple that could be purchased for a price at the Black Diamond Saloon.

Well, he wasn't about to go looking for "love" by any definition, Lester concluded as he picked himself up off the ground and proceeded toward the cook's shanty, pointedly ignoring the nearby 'jacks. If the Lord had a woman in mind for him, then he'd just have to make it so plain that he'd have to be blind not to see her!

Even as Lester sat down to a tin plate piled high with stew, a huge buttered hard roll, and steaming mug of coffee, he could not push away the disturbing thoughts. Instead, into his mind came the beguiling visions of several young women he had known. But why, oh why, did the image of pretty, well-scrubbed faces, neatly coiffed hair, and well-bred deportment lose out to the memory of a flaming-haired, sloe-eyed, filthy girl named Joy, who was anything but a joy to be around?

Lester shook his head as if to clear it, feeling something akin to fear. A sense of impending disaster.

Sighing heavily, he looked heavenward, unmindful of the lumberjacks who jostled around him at a nearby table. "Not her, Lord," Lester whispered helplessly, his lips scarcely moving behind the coffee mug, his breath sending the warm vapor filming up around his eyes. "I think I'd rather you strike me dead than inflict such tribulation upon me. Anyone but her, Lord . . . *please!* After all, Joy ain't even a Christian. Surely you don't want me to be unequally yoked with a heathen!

"Please keep in mind that Joy doesn't cotton to me any better than I do to her, and it'd take a passel of miracles to change our feelings, I'm thinkin'. And, Lord, if you'll pardon me for being a mite cheeky, Sir, I'd just as leave you'd keep those 'miracles' to yourself! One miracle's all I'm really needin' . . . to find and possess the perfect *horse*. . . ."

chapter
8

MIN-O-TA WAS WEARY with her struggle to comprehend her strange surroundings when the blanket of night fell again, and she was shown once again to the room where she had spent the previous night, curled up on the floor. To her confused mind, it had seemed a lifetime before. Yet logic told her that all that had drained her from too much thinking and straining to answer had occurred since the woman with the name of a flower had come to her room well after first light.

As Min-O-Ta stumbled sleepily into the room, assisted by the young one called Becky Rose, who clucked and fussed over her, the morning's sequence returned to play through her mind as vividly as when it had first happened.

"Are you awake, Joy?" the older one had inquired as she swept into the room, crossing to the window to draw back the curtains and allow the sunlight to drive out the darkness.

Assuming that since there was no one else in the room with them, the woman was addressing her, she had grunted a response.

"Rise and shine, Joy dear," Rose trilled, then paused to translate her usual morning chatter into halting Chippewa.

Reluctantly Min-O-Ta got to her feet, clutching the voluminous cotton nightdress around her slim form, brushing masses of tangled red hair from her tanned cheeks as the flower woman continued in her chirpy voice, saying words that were not understood.

"I'm goin' to fetch some water so you can take a sponge bath. That's all you'll really need, considerin' the dousin' we gave you last night at Marissa's house."

Min-O-Ta's ankles and knees felt stiff and they crackled as she was led across the hardwood floor to a washbasin, where she stood shivering, more from nervousness than the morning chill.

"I'll be right back," Rose assured, "with hot water, linens, and a bar of lye soap."

Though Min-O-Ta could not make out the words, the woman's meaning was clear, for when she returned, she was carefully balancing a pitcher of hot water. Fluffy white linens were neatly folded over her forearm.

"Now, wash up, child," Rose invited with appropriate gestures. And when Min-O-Ta made no move to comply, she lathered a cloth and began to demonstrate, straining to recall the Chippewa.

Rose was just applying the towel to Joy's arm, buffing until her skin pinkened and tingled, when there was a rap on the door.

"Did you find something for Joy to wear, Becky?" Rose called over her shoulder.

"I believe so," replied the hotel owner's daughter who was about the same size as Min-O-Ta.

"Then stick around and help me dress her, dear. I expect she'll put up as much fuss as a newborn babe. Raised as she has been, it's goin' to take a spell to get the hang of things in the civilized world."

"I'll help, Mama," Becky agreed, smiling hesitantly at Joy, whose solemn expression never changed.

After what seemed like an eternity of fumbling, tugging, and straining to fasten the stubborn buttons and snaps, Rose and Becky had Joy suitably attired to appear downstairs in public. And the two accompanied the white-Indian girl down the flight of stairs, walking cautiously beside her as Joy wobbled about on Marissa's cast-off slippers.

Tantalizing odors wafted from the dining room and Joy was willingly led in and seated at a table by the window.

There was cutlery neatly laid out at Joy's place, but the girl ignored the heavy, ornate silverware and began plucking up tidbits of food with her hands, shoving it into her mouth until her cheeks bulged like a chipmunk's. She chewed a time or two, then swallowed, bolting down her food as Rose and Becky looked on in silent dismay.

"Ma!" Becky gasped, unable to contain herself a moment longer when the girl picked up the china plate and licked it clean. "She has the manners of a sow!"

"Shush!" Rose ordered, grateful that Joy could not yet understand them. "Don't judge, darlin'. She hasn't had the same upbringing you have, you know. Why, if we'd been brought up with Indians, we'd be doin' the selfsame things."

Becky stared at the strange girl who must be nearly her age, overwhelmed by the enormity of her dilemma. "But how are we ever going to teach her all she needs to know, Mama?"

Rose sighed. "One day at a time, and with a lot of love and a heap o' patience. Although she's almost a full-grown lass, we'll have to instruct her as if she were a wee child. Young'uns catch on quick-like, and I'm sure she will, too, if we're mindful to set the proper example."

"I'll do my best," Becky promised.

"Somehow I knew you would, dear," Rose murmured. "Now, what is that old sayin' about a picture bein' worth a thousand words? Maybe Joy'll get the idea better if she sees a

demonstration. You can start right now by eatin' your breakfast and showin' her how."

Rose and Becky were aware of Joy's watching the hotel
owner's daughter as she retrieved her knife and fork and cut
the breakfast sausage patty into bite-size pieces, daintily wiping her lips with a napkin regularly throughout the meal.

"I think she's goin' to be a quick study," Rose said when
Joy picked up her own utensils and haltingly followed suit.

Her stomach full, a warm cup of coffee cupped in her
hands, the girl's face lost its guarded expression and ventured
a weak grin. It was as if she had never smiled before and
wasn't sure quite how to manage it.

"Not only is she going to be a quick study, Mama . . . I
think Joy is going to be my *friend!*"

"Praise God for that," Rose murmured, daring to give
Joy's shoulder an affectionate pat.

"Maybe she could keep me company today as I do my
chores," Becky suggested.

"A good idea." Rose nodded approvingly. "She's not
much of a talker. See if you can help her learn a few simple
words today. Practice them with her, darlin', like you'd help
one of the young'uns with their multiplication tables."

"That could be almost like a game."

"Learnin's easier when it's fun," Rose said. "And if you
have a problem and need some help, I can try to translate, or
we can wait 'til Homer comes home from his business trip to
Warroad." She gazed off into the distance with a dreamy look
in her eyes. "I'm lookin' forward to his return. I want him to
talk to Joy, and I don't mind sayin' I'd like a little time with
him myself. . . . We have some plans to make."

Becky went through her workday, chatting with Joy,
expecting no responses, but using her daily routine as an

occasion to teach. Holding up various objects—a vase, a plate, a bowl of flowers—Becky carefully pronounced each word, touching the article so that Joy could associate the name with it. And by the time they had finished their evening meal, Joy had added five new words to her vocabulary.

"Do you think you could help Joy prepare to retire by yourself, Becky?" Rose asked. "I'm dreadfully tired. And she seems to really cotton to you."

"I'll be glad to, Ma," Becky agreed. "In fact, I've been thinking. . . . Maybe in another day or two, Joy would like to share my room. It's big enough so we could squeeze in another bed and chest of drawers. She might feel better with some company."

Rose gave her daughter an admiring glance. "That's right thoughtful, Becky, and I daresay she'd welcome the notion . . . later. But right now, with so much to take in, I warrant she'd appreciate a little privacy."

She watched her daughter and the white-Indian girl progress up the staircase. Although Joy would soon be a grown woman, Rose couldn't help noticing that now, visibly tired after her long day, she trailed after Becky Rose much like her younger siblings used to follow in the wake of their big sister.

Rose was just finishing up in the kitchen when Becky reappeared downstairs. "She's sleeping," she whispered, so as not to risk waking the newcomer. "I stayed with her 'til she drifted off. I pointed out the bed, but she chose to sleep on the floor."

"Give her time," Rose quietly suggested. "Right now, the hard floor is familiar . . . so that's a small comfort to her, though I figure that before long she'll be lookin' for a softer spot."

JOY IN THE MORNING

"She no longer seems so bumfuzzled by our garments," Becky said. "This morning, the way she kept tripping over her skirt and tugging at her bodice, I thought she would rip the dress apart at the seams with her hitchings and tuggings."

Rose chuckled. "She's doing a right commendable job, I'd say. It can't be easy. Heavens! Just imagine how hard it'd be for us to have to take up Indian ways after a lifetime of knowin' only our own. What a blow it must've been for her poor mama, kidnapped by savages. . . ."

"I do wonder what kind of story she could tell," mused Becky, her eyes wide. "I'll bet it's a doozy."

Rose shook her head. "'Tis my hope that Homer will be able to find out soon enough, for the more we know about the girl . . . the better able we'll be to help her."

"She's so pretty, too . . . but I don't think she knows it."

"Probably not," Rose said with a shrug. "Maybe the way she looks made her feel downright ugly if she compared herself with the other people in the tribe."

"Well, it's time she learned how to look like a white girl instead of an Indian!" Becky ventured, sounding surprisingly determined.

Rose looked up in surprise. "You have something in mind?"

"Reckon I do," Becky admitted in an airy voice. "If Joy will hold still long enough, I'm going to experiment on her hair with the curling iron I purchased at the mercantile. I'd like to braid it and put it up in a coronet, then curl some little tendrils to frame her face. She has lovely features, you know."

"When you're through with her, she'll be purty as a picture, Becky Rose."

"Pretty enough to turn heads when she walks into church with us on Sunday morning," Becky said with smug satisfaction.

"You think she'll agree to go? 'Cause I'll admit, the idea crossed my mind, but I didn't think we had a chance." Sighing heavily, Rose blurted out her newest worry. "She's been askin' for the medicine bag. Actually, demandin' I return it to her. I'm afraid she's placed all her faith in that smelly little leather bag on a rawhide thong!"

Silence spiraled until the tick-tock of the grandfather clock in the parlor was clearly audible.

"But Ma, you've got to understand . . . that's all she's known," Becky reminded her mother.

"Well, I feel sorry for the poor thing. 'Tisn't her fault she's a pagan. But I haven't the conscience to give it back when it ain't right, plain as day!"

"But it's *hers*, Ma," Becky said, her tone soft.

"I know that, Becky Rose. But *I* also know it's a form of pagan worship. Maybe even idolatry!"

"We can lead her to Christ, Mama, but we can't force her to a take him as her own."

Rose was still adamant. "Well, I'm not goin' to let her think *I* believe in such things!"

"What if by snatching away her talisman—which *we* know can't help her—she hardens her heart against the true Savior, who *can?* She could end up rejecting him out of pure resentment toward us for forcing our ways on her."

Rose frowned. "I hadn't thought of it quite like that."

"But . . . I could be wrong," Becky said, her tone hesitant. She lowered her eyes. "Wh–when Pa used to try to keep you from going to church, and us children, too . . . it only made me all the more determined to go."

Rose nodded with sudden understanding. "You're thinkin' that if I let her have that smelly leather bag to hang around her neck, she'll be more prone to give it up of her own volition? Exchange it someday for a true and lastin' faith?"

"Yes. At least we can hope and pray she will."

"And we could look through the Sears and Roebuck catalog and see if we can find a pretty gold necklace with a cross pendant," Rose added with growing enthusiasm. "'Course, a piece of jewelry doesn't have magical powers, but it could help take the place of that smelly old charm. Besides, every time she looks at herself in the mirror, she'd think of what Jesus did for her on the cross and that he's the One who'll protect her."

Becky nodded happily. "What a wonderful idea, Mama!"

"Just to be safe, that's one more thing I'm aimin' to discuss with Homer when he returns from his trip." Rose sighed again. "I had hoped that man would have shown up by now. Reckon his business has detained him. What we have to discuss will just have to wait," she finished sadly.

Becky put her arm around her mother and gave her a fond embrace, her eyes twinkling. "From what you've said, Mama, it's waited many, many years . . . so what's one more day?"

"Only twenty-four hours," Rose said, smiling softly. "But mark my words, Daughter, when you're in love with a man, one day apart can seem like a thousand years." A frown suddenly overtook the gentle features. "And when you ain't in love with a bloke, girl, each day together can seem just as long. . . ."

chapter
9

Min-O-Ta's mind was whirling by the time she was ready to creep upstairs to her quarters in the large tepee, the molted feather of a bluejay and a pinch of soot from the wood range in the kitchen, secreted in a rag she had located in the pantry. Holding the rag behind her, she crossed to the lobby where the flower woman was standing and hesitantly touched her arm.

Rose was dressed to go out for the evening, accompanied by Becky Rose. Min-O-Ta offered them a shy, sleepy smile. Then, for extra credibility, she stifled a yawn and motioned toward the upstairs sleeping room where she had spent her nights since coming here.

"Sleep well, darlin'." The flower woman's words were spoken softly and kindly and, though they were not understood, her quick hug was.

Becky Rose waggled her fingers in a gesture of farewell. "See you tomorrow, Joy."

Slowly, as if she were exhausted, Min-O-Ta trudged up the stairs where the carpeting was worn thin from the steps of many feet. When she had cleared the second landing and heard the front doors close behind the flower woman and her daughter, decorum fled. Min-O-Ta catapulted ahead, skidded around a corner, raced for her room and closed the door quickly behind her. Then, in the dim light of the lamp, she looked around the room, her expression determined.

What to take? She'd have to travel light. If only she had her medicine bag!

She fumed further at the thought of doing without her buckskins and moccasins and looked down in disgust at the white woman's garment that covered her lean frame from ankle to neck. With a Chippewa word spat in disgust, she kicked off the shoes that had imprisoned her feet without mercy all day long. The soles of her feet remained tough, and Min-O-Ta realized that she would fare better barefoot than reduced to hobbling along in the ridiculous foot coverings!

There was nothing to do about the garments. She hadn't time to scour the premises for her buckskins. Besides, the way the women had carried on about their musky scent, they had probably burned the clothes by now. Or they might still be sozzling somewhere in a tub of hot water, strong with lye soap.

Still looking about the room for anything she might need, Min-O-Ta had a moment to consider her lot. Jake had sold her to the yellow-haired lady's brother, who had given her to the pretty woman. Now it appeared that she had been passed off to the smiling woman with the name of a flower. This one seemed pleasant enough, but what if the flower woman also tired of her . . . and gave her away? What if it was to someone like Jake . . . or worse still . . . the dark-eyed savage, Billy LeFave?

All Min-O-Ta wanted was her freedom. She must escape!

When she had first considered the idea, the plight of captives who fled the tribal community filled her with alarm. Such prisoners were hunted down, and upon their return were treated worse than before. It was a fearful prospect.

Still, with her knowledge of the woods, her basic skills, her stout heart, Min-O-Ta was sure she could take care of herself,

JOY IN THE MORNING

eke out an existence and, perhaps, make her own way in the world as she and Jake had done.

She knew that her captors would be looking for a red-haired woman. All she could hope to do was confuse them . . . at least for a time.

Edging close to the glass behind the chunky wooden contraption in the corner, she drew the lamp closer, and in its flickering light, carefully applied soot to her eyebrows with the tip of the feather. The effect was dramatic. Squinting carefully, she darkened her lashes, too. There. Except for her tresses, which still shone like burnished copper, the change was remarkable.

Having noticed the women's headdresses hanging from pegs near the back door of the cooking area, an idea formed. She would cover her hair so that no one could tell its color! And in what was surely a sudden stroke of genius, she scraped the soot together with her fingernail and began to apply it deftly to the juncture where her hair grew in a heart-shaped peak above her forehead.

With her disguise complete, Min-O-Ta was ready to depart. Where she would go she did not know, only that she needed to flee as quickly as possible.

She paused only long enough to rumple the bedclothes that Becky Rose had shown her how to make in guest rooms, an art she had quickly mastered. Then, frowning in thought, she grabbed a pillow and a spare frock from a peg on the wall and shoved the garment beneath the coverlet, carefully shaping it so that, at a glance, it would appear that she was sleeping.

That should give her until dawn. And by then she would be far, far away, leaving no trail for them to follow.

Min-O-Ta's heart was thundering in her chest as she crept down the stairway, relieved that no one was in the lobby.

113

Instead of boldly exiting the front doors, where she would risk being discovered, she slipped out the back door, pausing only long enough to let her eyes adjust to the darkness.

Familiar night sounds greeted her, giving her an odd sense of comfort. The song of the cricket. The low thrumming of frogs in a swamp somewhere. Even the pesky drone of mosquitoes was welcome to her ears.

Min-O-Ta slipped into the shadows, waiting once more to get her bearings and determine what course she should take. The decision seemed ready-made, for she heard a horse-drawn wagon rumbling up a side street. From the raucous sounds coming from its driver, she knew he was under the spell of firewater. She would not ask for a ride. She would simply steal it, and the unsuspecting teamster would be none the wiser.

The dewy grass was cool and soothing on Min-O-Ta's bare feet, hot and swollen from the constraints of shoes. The loose sand at the edge of the street was fine as talc, a balm to her soles. She realized that she would leave tracks but trusted that they would scarcely be distinguishable from the prints left by the village youths.

Min-O-Ta's eyes quickly adjusted to the nighttime gloom, and she could readily make out the silhouette of the drunken teamster slumped behind the reins of a spring-seat wagon. Her breath quickened and her heart thudded, knowing that the moment to make her move was at hand.

Clutching up the awkward skirts, once again wishing for her buckskins, she shot toward the rear of the wagon, running low and hugging the ground, as she'd been taught by the Chippewa when little more than a tot. The horses paid her no heed as they plodded along, heads bobbing, harnesses jingling, tails switching.

The driver, so in his cups that he was oblivious to his surroundings, apparently didn't hear the faint thud Min-O-Ta made as she grabbed the wagon slats with her hands and hoisted herself up, bracing her feet against the base of the conveyance. She drew in a deep breath, kept her arms rigid, and crouched low. Thus concealed from the driver and hidden from the view of all but those with eyesight as sharp as her own, she settled in for a ride that would take her as far as the teamster had a notion to travel.

It didn't matter in which direction he took her . . . as long as it was far from the flinty-faced man who had purchased her, only to find her not to his liking.

As they bounced along northward, Min-O-Ta felt herself doze off, even though her fingers never relaxed their grip on the wagon slats. Nor did her feet lose their curled-toed clutch on the base of the wagon, ensuring her against the likelihood of being dislodged as they clattered over deep ruts and potholes.

Min-O-Ta had no idea just how far the teamster had progressed north and west of the town—judging from the constellations gleaming in the velvety night sky—but he wasn't making the horse step high and smart. The lazy beasts were scarcely moving, meandering along an aimless path, it seemed.

When she realized she had heard no grunts or muttered curses in quite awhile, Min-O-Ta pursed her lips and whistled like a night bird. Just as she suspected: The sound raised no reaction from the driver. He was fast asleep!

Before another half-mile had passed, the horses, feeling that the reins had gone slack, veered toward the edge of the trail and within another moment or two had come to a full halt. The stillness was broken only by the sound of their flat teeth ripping off blades of lush grass and the clanking of their bits as they chewed, swallowed, and occasionally stomped or switched at a nocturnal insect.

Min-O-Ta wished that she dared to take the reins herself, but she feared being discovered. And with a sigh, she hopped down from the wagon, wincing when she landed on a hard-packed rut. She was momentarily tripped up by her skirts before falling forward, clutching at the wagon and getting a splinter in the palm of her hand for her effort.

Shaking her stinging hand, she picked herself up off the ground and set out on foot, guided by the North Star above. She was weary but lighthearted over the ease of her escape. Nothing—and no one—would get in her way until she had reached the sandy beaches of the southern shores of the Lake of the Woods.

By the time Lester had scraped his plate clean of stew, wiped up the remaining gravy with a crust of sourdough bread, and savored the last of his steaming hot coffee, he wanted nothing more than to locate an unused bunk so he could rest his aching bones. Not only that, he was tired of suspecting that he was the topic of speculation on the part of the lumberjacks in the camp. He was about to give in to the urge to escape to the bunkhouse when another burst of laughter erupting from a nearby table made him cringe inwardly.

Lester got busy neatly stacking his plate, cutlery, and coffee mug, lingering to discern the reason for their ribald guffaws. Picking up enough to satisfy himself that his suspicions were correct, he swallowed hard, choking on a lump of unpleasant emotions lodged in his throat. They *were* making sport of him, no doubt aware of the humiliating auction that had resulted in his acquisition, not of a spirited sorrel mare but of a redheaded spitfire who didn't like him one whit better than he liked her!

Now he knew that there was no way he could remain in the lumber camp overnight—and keep his dignity and temper intact. It seemed inevitable that if he stayed around the lumberjacks, who battled not only with weariness but with boredom, he'd have to endure their ragging. In the few months he'd been with the company, Lester had observed a few other unfortunates who'd been the butt of their cruel jokes. He had never joined in the malicious fun and was always relieved that *he* wasn't their target. This time he was. . . .

Lester had felt the strain building over the past day or two and knew that he was testy to the point that, if he was teased, he'd strike like an out of sorts rattlesnake. At the same time, he was aware that he couldn't begin to hold his own in a scuffle with the average lumberjack.

Most of the men sitting around him were huge—massive shoulders, bulging biceps, steel-hard stomachs, legs like portico columns, and hands the size of Virginia hams. Any one of the 'jacks could snap Lester in two as if he were a slat of kindling.

Deciding that discretion was the better part of valor, Lester made his decision to leave. He'd a lot rather spend a night being stung by pesky insects than suffering the needling of a group of ignorant lumberjacks!

Without a word, Lester deposited his used dinnerware on the stack of dirty dishes mounding in a metal washtub. Then he walked over to a nearby kitchen worker with a huge apron secured around his massive belly—proof that he sampled his own creations—and asked, "Can you spare a little something for my breakfast, Cookie?"

"Sure, son!" said the round-faced man, swiping at his double chin and leaving a dusting of flour on his darkly stubbled cheek.

Nodding his thanks, Lester helped himself to a few corn muffins and a leftover cathead biscuit.

Another cook standing nearby let out a laugh that sounded like the bray of a donkey. "Don't tell me that woman of your'n cain't cook, bub!" he called out in fake astonishment, chuckling into the kettle he was scouring. "Sure got hornswoggled, didn't ye? 'Spect it'll take awhile to save up for a replacement at those fancy prices!"

"Oh, so this is the feller, is it?" said the first cook, as much to himself as to the other. "Well, well, . . ." And he peered at Lester with such curiosity that Lester's skin felt crawly.

"A man can forgive a woman a lot o' failin's—includin' bein' ugly—if she can set a good table," said a nearby lumberjack, scratching through his thick beard. "On the other hand, a bloke might be inclined to overlook certain defects . . . iffen she's appealin' to the eyes. And I hear tell your gal looks like somethin' the cat dragged in!"

"Oh, now that's not a fair appraisal," another 'jack defended. "I talked to a feller who was on the scene, and he figgers Lester overpaid for her, but he also opines she'll clean up right nice."

It was worse than Lester had even imagined it might be. Blocking the crude comments, he strode woodenly from the room, leaving a tidal wave of laughter in his wake.

It seemed like an endless journey from the hot, stuffy dining room into the cool of the evening. But here, the crisp air felt like a soothing poultice on his burning cheeks. Still, he was grateful that there had been few company officials to witness his humiliation.

Lester was also grateful for the full moon that illuminated his way as he followed a well-marked trail, beaten smooth of grass, briars, and debris by the passage of many a man and horse dragging logs from the deep forest. Farther from camp, the trail was less clearly marked, and he lost his footing several times, falling heavily.

He was wheezing mosquitoes from his nostrils and spitting them from his mouth by the time Lester concluded that he ought to stop and build a fire to discourage the night-flying insects. And when he stumbled into a small clearing in the woods and heard the lyrical sound of a bubbling stream, he dropped to the ground and clawed together some dry debris. Drawing a match from his tin container, he brought a flame flaring. Carefully he fed the fire until he had a comfortable blaze going. The sparks shot up into the night air, with the hazy smoke collecting in a cloud that held at bay a swarm of mosquitoes humming angrily just outside the billowing perimeter of protection.

For a long while Lester leaned against the rough bark of a jackpine tree, whose fallen needles provided a soft cushion beneath him. He was tired and would have relished dropping off to sleep. Instead, he found his mind churning once more with thoughts he'd entertained earlier about life, love, and his purpose in God's plan.

It seemed to Lester that he had fallen asleep only moments before when a hovering mosquito, which had zigzagged through the remaining smoky defense, stung him on the cheek. Half asleep, he slapped at it, rudely awakening himself to a newly broken dawn.

Birds twittered overhead, creating a peaceful chorus for the serene stillness of the morning. Sunlight filtered through the thick pine boughs, creating dappled patterns on the ground.

For a moment Lester basked in the beauty around him, content to lie there . . . until he remembered the previous day and night.

With a sigh he boosted himself from the ground, stretched, and stirred through the ashes to assure himself that the embers were completely dead before breaking camp.

When his stomach growled, he remembered the cold muffins he'd wangled from the cook and drew them out of his knapsack, bolting them down. He cupped his hand to drink from the stream, rinsing his face and drying it on the sleeve of his shirt. Then when he had run his damp fingers through his dark blond hair, he abandoned the campsite deep in the big wood and set out, walking due east.

Each time he came to a creek, he lapped up a few sips of water and cooled his warm face, rinsing away the salty sweat. Gauging the rising sun and estimating where he believed himself to be, he reckoned that it would be half a day of steady walking before he left the wilderness and came out on a road sufficiently well-traveled to hitch a ride to town.

As Lester's stomach began to rumble with more frequency, a startled jackrabbit bounded out of the brush, almost directly underfoot. At the sight, he promised himself that before much longer, he'd unholster his pistol and shoot either a hare or a squirrel. He'd skin it out, wash the cleaned carcass in a brook, and then affix it to a spit of green saplings to roast over a small campfire. It might not taste as good as Ma's wild game—roasted until the meat was dripping juices and tender to the touch—but it would serve to ease the gnawing ache of hunger in the pit of his belly.

The noonday sun was soaring high in the sky when Lester squeezed off a shot. The report seemed thunderous in the still woodlands. The pistol recoiled against his palm as the rabbit arched into the air, then flopped sideways, lying still in its tracks.

Within half an hour, the hare was roasting on the spit. As aromas grew more tantalizing and the meat sizzled and hissed over the dancing flames, Lester found that his mood had improved and he enjoyed his meal and the moment of respite before he moved on again.

Lester felt optimistic—almost euphoric—as he kicked dirt over the coals and then set out at a brisk pace, his body and spirit rejuvenated by the rest and repast.

Even so, another two hours of steady walking left Lester feeling tired and testy. What had started out as a pleasant day in the woods was fast becoming a test of endurance through a natural obstacle course. Adding to his general misery was the fact that mosquitoes had discovered his presence again and seemed to have spread word of his whereabouts to their cohorts.

Lester was tense and tight-lipped from the frustration of swatting at mosquitoes, stumbling through tangles of brush, and halting abruptly to disengage razor-sharp briars from his skin, clothes, and scalp. And when he saw ahead of him a windrow created by fallen trees that appeared to have been uprooted by a twister, and bramble patches knotted to the earth, stretching a great distance in both directions, his heart sank. Surveying the situation, he felt like slamming his fist into the nearest tree.

He decided to face what appeared to be the lesser of the two evils: the high, wide maze of fallen trees in various stages of decomposition—jackpines, balm o' Gileads, a tamarack, and a birch or two. But by the time Lester had picked and chosen his way from rotting limb to decaying trunk, he was questioning the wisdom of his choice to avoid the bramble patches in order to spare himself a few more scratches and abrasions.

Lester's outlook improved a bit, however, when he realized that he'd almost successfully negotiated the massive deadfall. Rather than inch his way down the steep slope of rotting branches, he decided to jump from his present vantage point, marshaling enough momentum to leap free of the debris so he'd land on solid ground.

As Lester poised to make the leap, his boot heel dislodged a rotting length of bark that shifted beneath his weight. In the act of jumping, his arms pinwheeled as he tried to counter the slip. Arms flailing for balance, he found nothing he could grab hold of to break his fall.

Instead of landing on level ground, Lester's point of impact was the very edge of the windrow, where smooth, rounded, age-weathered stobs nestled. The force of his leap was such that decaying branches rolled away, and he landed awkwardly, staggering, as the debris was dislodged from its resting place.

He was about to regain his balance when he took a hitching step. Here, instead of solid earth, he encountered matted grass obscuring some animal's burrow, tunneled beneath the deadfall.

Lester's right foot slammed through the thin matting of grass and into the hole, and he yelped in pain as he landed with a spine-jarring thud. A searing, white-hot ache seemed to bolt from ankle to thigh. A wave of nausea rolled over him, and he took a deep breath.

Resting for a moment before trying to extricate his leg from the hole, Lester wiped his sleeve across his brow that was damp with cold sweat. "O Lord, please don't let it be broke," he whispered in near despair.

Gritting his teeth against the grinding pain, he slowly placed his weight on his hands, feeling the bark cut into his palms. He flexed his shoulders, easing his limb from the earthen trap. Grabbing a nearby sapling, he gripped it, tugging himself upright. He tested his toes before trying to put his weight on his right leg. It hurt. But at least he could stand on it.

"Thank God," he sighed. "It ain't broke after all."

chapter
10

THE TEAKETTLE ON the wood range let out a few piercing shrills in accompaniment to Dr. Marcus Wellingham's cheery whistle as he made his way from the master bedroom to the infirmary.

Marissa, who had dragged herself from bed half an hour earlier to fix a breakfast tray for the sickroom, drew her fingers through her hair and yawned, shaking her head as if to clear the grogginess from her mind. Marc had had less sleep than she, and she marveled that her husband could arise from his bed and instantly be alert and ready for the challenges of the day.

There were times, especially now, as the infant growing beneath her heart moved restlessly, that Marissa envied Marc's capacity to fall asleep almost the moment he laid his head on his pillow. She had figured it must be an ability learned while in medical school that had served him well during his internship and residency.

Nowadays it seemed that she lay awake more than ever, tossing and turning. Marc had explained that the bones and vertebrae of her spinal column created a lumpy surface for their baby, so discomfort sometimes awakened the infant to activity when Marissa most needed her rest.

She had intended to stroll over to the Grant Hotel to see how Joy was doing but hadn't the energy. Therefore, she'd had to be content with the scant news brought by Maggie

Grant, Rose's youngest child, who reported on the white-Indian girl's progress.

Billy LeFave had been the lone occupant of the infirmary for several days now, at least until the evening before when a logger had brought in his pregnant wife who was threatening to go into early labor. But toward midnight, her mild pangs had ceased as abruptly as they had begun. And shortly before dawn, Marc, whose sleep had been interrupted at regular intervals during the night, had deemed the incident a false alarm.

Now the young matron, Mrs. Olson, was waiting until after breakfast when Dr. Wellingham would give her a ride home so her husband would not have to lose a day's work.

More than ever, Marissa was thankful that Marc had Harmony to assist him. She herself had undertaken to learn nursing techniques to help out, but with the addition to their family soon, she had been forced to rest more often. Her advancing pregnancy had robbed her of energy in ways she had not anticipated, and she was more than grateful to relinquish her own duties to another who was so trustworthy and meticulous.

Marissa had always known that the daughter of Lizzie and Harmon Childers was a special person. Even as a child in the one-room schoolhouse where she had received most of her education, Harmony had shown exceptional intelligence and responsibility. Still, on those occasions when she could be cajoled into merrymaking, Lizzie's only girl was delightful company.

Marissa's assessment of Harmony Childers was one shared by her husband. Marc viewed Harmony as an exemplary nurse—practical, forthright, observant, and intuitive—qualities she had quite naturally acquired at her mother's side.

Now these traits served her well in her chosen profession. It was Marissa's further belief that had it been possible for Harmony to attend medical school, she herself would have made an excellent physician.

Marissa was jolted from these musings when she heard her husband, his whistle preceding him into the kitchen. "How are the patients this morning?" she inquired with a bright tone that belied the weariness she felt.

She boosted herself from the table and went to the wood range, forcing lightness into her step as she fetched the coffeepot and poured Marc a cup, then took a seat across from him.

He whisked a crisp, linen napkin into place on his lap before replying, "Mrs. Olson is finishing up her breakfast and champing at the bit to return home, if I don't miss my guess. LeFave's holding his own."

"I'm glad to hear it."

Marc stirred cream in his coffee and added one lump of sugar, then shook his head in wonderment. "By all rights . . . LeFave should be a dead man."

Marissa set a plate of French toast, sausage, fried potatoes, and eggs in front of him. "He's not out of the woods yet, is he?"

"No . . . not really . . . though, so far, he doesn't appear to be septic. But time will tell. At present, LeFave is progressing beyond my most optimistic expectations. I have an idea he'll make it, poor as other physicians might consider his chances."

There was a certainty in Marc's declaration that caused Marissa to look up. She'd grown quite proficient at reading her husband's face, gauging a patient's progress even before he had uttered the words. This time was no different. "How can you be so sure?"

Marc's level gaze met hers across the table. "Because Harmony Childers won't let him die. . . ."

"She *has* nursed him tirelessly, hasn't she?" Marissa murmured as she poured her husband a fresh cup of coffee and sat down again to sip her tea and nibble at a piece of toast dripping with peach marmalade.

"Yes, she has." Marc shot his wan wife a pointed look. "And so have you."

Marissa shrugged off his compliment. "I've done little, darling, except to keep vigil at his bedside . . . and that mainly to spell Harmony."

He nodded. "LeFave's been in critical condition, constantly in crisis. I really must find another young woman and train her as a nurse to free you more, darling."

"Oh, I haven't hurt myself any," she insisted. "I only sit in a chair and read to him from the Good Book while I watch for signs of a setback so I can alert you or Harmony."

"Praise God, his physical health seems to be improving. But," Marc dropped his voice, fearful of being overheard, even this far from the infirmary, "if his spiritual condition isn't healed . . . it's only a matter of time before he's involved in an altercation from which he won't walk away. And this should have been just such an incident, although for some reason it was not."

"There's a purpose, isn't there, Marc?" Marissa asked quietly. "That Billy is still alive, I mean."

"My sentiments exactly, my dear. I have faith that the Lord is allowing us to help save Billy LeFave's life because, in some way, even his rude existence is important."

Marissa felt a helpless shiver run through her. "I know—from personal experience—that the Lord can bring good from evil."

For a moment, memories paraded through her mind. How Miss Abby, in her demented state, had been snookered out of the family property from which they were evicted by the two rogues who had spirited Marissa off to Chicago. But these very events, tragic though they were, had led her to Marc in what some would have called a chance encounter. Nevertheless, it was one Marissa would always believe had been planned by God himself since the foundations of the world, for her life once more was filled with grace and blessing.

She could not resist advancing a theory. "Perhaps it's only a matter of time before Billy finds Christ as his Savior."

The sudden furrow on Marc's forehead revealed that he thought the possibility highly unlikely. "To be frank, Marissa, as selfless as Harmony is in caring for LeFave, I'm wondering if she might be . . . attracted . . . to the man."

Marissa, taken by surprise, almost choked on her tea. "Don't be ridiculous, Marc!" she said, the words coming out somewhere between a giggle and a gasp.

He arched a brow. "Am I?"

"Well, I should certainly hope so!"

"But isn't Harmony at an age when most young women begin to look around for someone who piques their romantic interest?"

Marissa snorted. "Harmony's too sensible for such flights of fancy! At least, she wouldn't be looking for the likes of a man like Billy LeFave!"

"We did promise Lizzie Mathews we'd take good care of her only daughter. I feel responsible for Harmony, my dear."

"Well, rest your mind, darling. I *know* her. Why she'd no more do a thing like that than . . ." Marissa broke off before she could add, "than *I* would!" for in the past, she had followed her foolish heart into some dire and desperate straits.

"We can't let her make a grave mistake," Marc said stubbornly.

"We won't. And we can count on Lester. He squabbles with Harmony, but it would be over his dead body if someone did her wrong!"

"True," Marc admitted. "But LeFave is a handsome man, in an almost sinister sort of way. And you know how some females can be about believing they can save a regular blighter from himself."

Marissa smiled at her husband. "Harmony may work to save his life. But I do believe she's wise enough not to sacrifice herself to save him from his misspent lifestyle. Think about it, Marc. They truly have nothing at all in common."

"Oh, I don't know about that. Several things come to mind."

"What in the world could they be?" she challenged.

Marc held up his hand to tick off the evidence. "Number one, they are red-blooded human beings. Number two, they are both still unmarried. Number three, they're lonely. Number four . . ."

"Don't be irritating, Marcus Wellingham!" Marissa warned, wrinkling her nose. "You know exactly what I mean! Why, they are as different as day and night . . . and I don't mean coloring alone, though that's a start, with Harmony as blond and fair as an Easter lily, and LeFave as dark and hard looking as . . . as a lump of coal! I'm sure, my dear husband, that deep down, Harmony finds the likes of Billy LeFave as repugnant as *I* do!"

Marc shrugged. "If so, then Harmony hides her feelings with more finesse than you do, darling."

"Oh, Marc, I simply see Billy LeFave as a poor suffering creature created in the image of the Lord, just like every other

129

person on the face of the earth. And I've steeled myself to treat him as I'd want to be treated."

Breaking off abruptly, Marissa sipped her tea lest she voice the illusive thoughts that taunted her like words on the tip of her tongue. What was it about Billy LeFave that intrigued her so? What she knew of his past was enough to give her pause at the idea of harboring a desperado in their midst.

Yet . . . there was something else about Billy that drew her to him like a moth to the flame. It was an odd niggling feeling she couldn't quite identify.

Of only one thing was she sure: She was not romantically attracted to the man. There was no room in her heart for anyone but Marc. Furthermore, she was equally convinced that Harmony wasn't interested in the darkly handsome rogue whom her husband, with his expert care, had pulled from the brink of death.

Still, Marc was right. There did seem to be something about LeFave that was causing Harmony to go above and beyond her usually fine nursing practices. And Marissa decided that when the young woman came in for her breakfast, she'd find a way to probe a bit and learn what her motives were. Perhaps by doing so, she might understand her own. . . .

That decision reached, Marissa didn't have long to wait.

Within the half hour, Marc had left the hospital with an ungainly and visibly tired Mrs. Olson in his custody. The logger's wife, who was a few years older than Marissa, was looking forward to returning home to her husband and children and biding her time until the babe reached full term.

Scarcely had the Wellingham horse clip-clopped down the street with Marc at the reins than Harmony drifted into the kitchen, yawning.

Marissa greeted her with a hug. "Good morning, dear,"

she said and smoothed a stray wisp of Harmony's blond hair into place. "Hungry?"

"Mmmm. . . ." Harmony frowned thoughtfully, as if taking inventory.

With a firm hand Marissa guided the slightly younger woman toward a chair at the table and Harmony collapsed into it gratefully. "At the moment, 'Rissa, I'm too tired to know. It was a long night with Mrs. Olson. Once the contractions stopped, she slept . . . but I'm afraid I didn't."

Marissa studied Harmony's features and decided that the young woman's cheeks were a whisper thinner than they'd been a few days earlier and a shade more wan. "You're hungry," Marissa decided for her. "One hot and nutritious breakfast coming right up."

"Well, I suppose I should eat a bite before I prepare some gruel and coax it down my patient's throat," Harmony admitted. "We must keep up Mr. LeFave's strength."

"And our own," Marissa added, as she dished up a sausage patty, fried potatoes, and piece of French toast from the warming oven.

Harmony's blue eyes, as discerning as her mother's, flicked up to assess the physician's wife with a practiced gaze. The faint wrinkle that marred her smooth brow seemed to signal that Harmony was not entirely happy with what she saw. "Maybe you should tend to your own health, Marissa, and the well-being of your coming little one," she admonished, "and let Dr. Wellingham and me see to the patients."

Marissa eased herself into a chair across the table from Harmony. "But I want to help, Harmony. Mr. LeFave— Billy—requires an inordinate amount of care right now. With such a severe wound, Marc fears sepsis." She shifted, seeking a more comfortable position. "I know your nursing duties are long and tiring, Harmony, but Marc has been talking about training another nurse to help you. It would certainly be more fair to you."

"Oh, I don't mind hard work. And it's worthwhile service and very rewarding," Harmony assured her, beginning to enjoy her meal.

"I know you don't mind, but Marc and I do. . . ." When the young nurse didn't reply, Marissa boldly steered the conversation in another direction. "Harmony . . . what is going on with Billy?" Marissa's voice was scarcely more than a spring breeze, riffling through the treetops.

Harmony looked up abruptly. "Why, whatever do you mean, 'Rissa?"

It was clear that the girl believed that Marissa was questioning the outcome of her husband's diagnosis or asking for an update on Billy's condition and not ferreting out the secrets of Harmony's heart, for the young woman's gaze was unwaveringly innocent, her tone unfaltering, and her cheeks devoid of even the faintest blush.

At this reaction, Marissa found herself blushing and stumbling over her own speech as she sought to clarify her intent. "Well . . . I . . . uh . . . it's just that you have been such a dutiful and devoted nurse to Billy LeFave that I–I'd begun to think there must be some personal reason," Marissa floundered. "That maybe you were in some way . . . *attracted* . . . to Mr. Lefave."

"Really?" Harmony was amused, then she grew pensive. "I suppose I'd have to admit that I've labored a bit harder than usual in Mr. LeFave's behalf. But, then, 'Rissa Wellingham, so have *you!*"

"I know," Marissa admitted, her tone almost desultory.

"The fact of the matter is that the man's wounds are very

serious," Harmony reminded her, "and you said yourself that Dr. Wellingham is fearful of some complication that could prove fatal despite all our best efforts."

"It's . . . more than that!" Marissa said, an edge of frustration creeping into her tone. "*Why?! Why* do we find ourselves so concerned over the likes of Billy LeFave?!"

Harmony's gaze dropped to the green plant serving as a centerpiece on the well-appointed round oak dining-room table. "Well . . . it's probably silly, and I can only speak for myself, Marissa," Harmony began in a quiet tone, "but it's as if by caring for Billy LeFave, I can pay off a debt of gratitude, long overdue."

"A debt? To whom?"

"To the kind folks who were there to help Grandpappy Alton when he was a wayfaring drifter and found himself sick or in need."

"Oh." Marissa's reply was a whisper. She hadn't expected to hear this simple, unselfish rationale.

"As a young lad," Harmony went on, "your pa was left with no living kin to turn to, and he hadn't yet learned that he could turn to the Lord. So he chose to walk the way of the world and provide for himself any way he could. Like it or not, 'Rissa, we must admit that the young Alton Wheeler, before Sue Ellen Stone came into his life, was a dead ringer for Billy LeFave, including his scandalous behavior in barrooms!"

"Of course . . . *Pa!*" Marissa breathed in an astonished whimper. "That's *it*, Harmony! I had no idea! I only knew something was drawing me to Billy LeFave, making me feel . . . soft, merciful, almost fond-like toward him, no matter that he's a reprobate and a rapscallion. But you're right . . . he *does* remind me of Pa."

"That's why I've been willing to work so hard to help save Billy's life, 'Rissa. Think for a minute just how much worse off this world would be if kind folks along the way hadn't taken pity on Alton Wheeler and given him a helping hand. Why, if they'd left Grandpappy to die, we'd never have seen what the Lord can do with a rascal."

"You're right." Marissa rubbed at the gooseflesh that suddenly rippled across her forearms.

"I was terribly fond of Grandpappy Alton," Harmony admitted. "Sometimes I even felt I came to know him in ways that his own daughters—you and Katie and Molly—did not."

"What do you mean?"

Harmony shrugged. "I was enough younger than you and Molly that I used to tag along with Jeremiah and Grandpappy Alton when Mama had things to do," she explained. "Sometimes I think they forgot I was there, and they'd talk about things the way men do. Don't be angry, 'Rissa, but I have good reason to believe that Alton Wheeler—in his worldly days—was every bit Billy LeFave's equal!"

Marissa frowned and gave a reluctant nod. "Now that you mention it, I remember some evenings at home, when we were sitting around the hearth and Pa was in a mood for reflecting, that he threw out a few bold hints about those days." She couldn't suppress a wry smile. "He warned us that we'd have to get up mighty early in the morning to ever pull the wool over his eyes, for he reckoned he'd done about all there was to do before Mama won his heart and the Lord won his soul."

"There's something about Mr. LeFave," Harmony began, "that makes me think he could become a godly man, too, if we don't give up on him. Maybe he's like a lump of coal,

Marissa, a diamond in the rough, and it'll take some terrible pressures before he can shine for the Lord."

For a moment Marissa was silenced, dazzled, by the simple logic and strong faith coming from Harmony's lips. It sounded like something her mama would have said, traits that were no doubt passed down from Lizzie Mathews—little-educated but blessed with common sense and divine wisdom. "Now that I think about it, Billy even resembles Pa in looks, doesn't he? Same coloring. A big, brawny man . . ."

"Grandpappy Alton always had a beard and Mr. LeFave is clean-shaven," Harmony interjected, "but he has the same ruddy coloring, the dark eyes, the bearing . . . sort of an untamed look about him."

"'Specially that wild cast to the eyes. We seldom saw it unless Pa was righteously riled. But I'm betting it was there more than once when he was a bitter, lonely man, living on the worldly side."

"Mr. LeFave's got that same glint in his eyes. I thought at first he was furious at being brought to the hospital from that tavern brawl. But maybe not. My feeling is," Harmony went on with rising excitement, "that when there's a fierce gleam in a person's eyes, what's actually glowing brightest is the flame-light of pure pain in the spirit."

"Well, Pa had plenty of pain in his life, that I know," Marissa said, sighing. "Abandonment. Confusion. Fear. A hunger to be loved and accepted. But, thank the Lord, before he passed on to his final reward, he also had a full measure of happiness."

"If Grandpappy Alton found peace and rest in the Lord, we can hope and pray that Billy LeFave will find it, too."

Big and brutal as he could be, relying on himself, Alton Wheeler had finally realized that turning to the Lord wasn't a confession of weakness but of strength. It hadn't been easy for Pa, Marissa knew. Nor had it been easy for Marissa herself, when in rebellion she had flung her beliefs aside and tasted briefly of what the world had to offer.

It wouldn't be easy for Billy LeFave, either.

"I have a hunch we're in for some interesting times in the days ahead," Marissa admitted with a sigh, even as her heart lifted over the prospect of Billy's change of heart.

"Right now, though, Mr. LeFave is too sick to protest." Harmony's mouth twisted in a wry smile. "When he regains consciousness . . . that's when we'll have our hands full."

"But we can do it," Marissa assured her with sudden optimism. "With our trust in God and his protection, there's nothing Billy LeFave can dish out that we can't handle."

"You're right."

"Of course I am," Marissa said lightly. "The Lord won't let us down now. But I'm Alton Wheeler's daughter through and through, and if Billy LeFave thinks he's going to get ornery as cat droppings with *me* . . . then he'd best be warned that there's enough of *Pa's* wild and woolly ways left in me that I may whup Billy LeFave over the head with a porcelain bedpan if he gives us any trouble!"

Harmony chuckled. "Then Mr. LeFave had certainly better mind his manners, 'Rissa. Or when he fully regains consciousness, instead of thanking Dr. Wellingham for saving his life, he may be begging him to protect him from the good doctor's *wife!*"

chapter
11

LESTER HOBBLED THROUGH the woods, wincing when he had to step down an incline to cross a shallow creek, gritting his teeth to bear the pain of levering up with his foot to crest the opposite bank. He remained on his feet, even the few times he stopped to rest, for he was aware that if he sat down, his ankle would immediately begin to swell.

Lester had had little experience with sprains. The one time in his life when he recalled suffering such an injury, Ma had bound his ankle with lengths of an old cotton bedsheet, and he'd been forced to cripple around the cabin with a rudely fashioned crutch Jeremiah had made for his stepson. Lester had remained in that condition for the better part of a week.

He seemed to recall his ma telling one of his brothers to "walk out" his sprain and he'd be "good as new in the morning." Lester wasn't sure "walking it out" was the right prescription for him, but as he had no choice in the matter, he kept on hiking, relieved when the pain did not grow any worse and merely settled in to become a numbing, throbbing thrum.

Lester was panting and sweating hard when he finally left the woods and knew that he was in the vicinity where he had hopped off the swing-dingle and entered the large tract of woodland. Traveling was easier on the well-defined trail. But with each step he took, he was increasingly convinced that he was most certainly not going to "walk out" the sprain and be as good as new in the morning. If anything, he would pay an added price for having subjected the limb to his weight. Still, he kept going, wondering how on earth he would find the strength and stamina to proceed in the face of the searing pain that shot upward the length of his leg.

He was in a remote area now, with the closest homesteader at least a mile away—about the distance he had estimated he was from the trail that cut through the wilderness and led to Lake of the Woods. Several smaller trails fanned out from here to allow access to homesteaders' cabins on the rugged plots of ground where they were carving homes for themselves out of the wilderness.

Minutes dragged by like hours. Lester continued to make his way east in hopes of connecting with the trail where, if nothing else, he could sit by the wayside and trust that sooner or later, someone would pass by and offer him a ride.

A half hour later, he shook his head, wrinkling his nose at an overpowering stench that wafted to him on the breeze, almost causing him to gag. Lester had almost no time to wonder what it was before he discovered its source. A black bear cub lay bloating in the woods, its tongue hanging from its mouth that gaped open in death, crusty spittle dried to a pasty foam on its muzzle. Blue-green blowflies buzzed around, frantic in their excited discovery of the feast.

"Wonder what killed that little fellow?" Lester murmured.

In the same instant the hair prickled at the nape of his neck as he wondered where its mama was. He looked around warily, almost weak with relief when he did not confront an angry bear.

"Maybe its mama met a sorry end," he reasoned, "and the poor little fellow wasn't able to survive on his own."

Lester moved on, away from the sickening smell. But he

continued to crane his neck, looking for a larger carcass in the vicinity. Not finding her body concerned him. If the mother had survived, it was reasonable to believe she might be near-by, hoping to nudge her motionless cub awake so they could go about their foraging.

Lester remained tense and on guard, for he well knew that a mother bear was a force to be reckoned with.

He heard no angry, threatening grunts, although some-where ahead in the woods there came rustlings followed by long moments of unbroken silence, when the hush of the for-est was undisturbed except for the warbling of songbirds and the crows' raucous cawing.

Cocking his ear in the direction of the disturbance, Lester began to skirt around to the north of the route the unseen beast seemed to be taking. His left hand gripped his walking stick, while he kept his right hand on the butt of his pistol. The handgun was a comfort, even though he realized that it was a most ineffective armament against a large bear—espe-cially an *angry* bear.

And as crippled as Lester was, his razor-sharp hunting knife, carried on a sheath dangling from his belt next to his hatchet, was of little use, too. Not that he'd have been enthu-siastic about the prospect of fighting a bear single-handedly like Davy Crockett and Dan'l Boone, whose stories had enthralled Lester since he was a pup.

He was sweating profusely by the time he made his way through the thick tangles of brush and realized he was within a hundred yards of where the trail intersected the deep woods.

In what had seemed a perverse game of cat-and-mouse, Lester had noticed that as he veered northward, the awkward, muffled noises seemed to follow. When he retraced his steps and lost ground by heading back west, the sounds were there, too, the distance between them remaining the same.

Finally, resolutely, knowing that he was rapidly losing his strength, Lester plunged straight ahead, intent on facing whatever it was that had filled him with dread. No sooner had he reached this decision, moving as the crow flies, than he immediately made out the form of a large black bear staggering through a thicket! She was huge. No doubt, the dead cub's mother.

The she-bear seemed disoriented, and for that Lester was grateful, though puzzled. For some reason, she had not caught his scent, though the wind should have blown it directly to her.

Then, almost as if she could read his thoughts, the bear turned listlessly, as if in slow motion. She lifted her leathery snout into the air, wheezed several times, then issued an out-of-sorts bellow that seemed to fall a bit short of outright fury. The sow stared at Lester, her inky eyes in the black fur making her gaze resemble two holes burnt in a black wool blanket.

Lester didn't realize he had been holding his breath from fright and tension until he exhaled, feeling limp and boneless as the air left his lungs. "God help me," he whispered. "O Lord . . . give me strength . . . show me what to do . . . protect me from that bear!"

Lester's faint prayer evolved into a chilling scream of terror when the black bear lowered her head and ambled toward him. For an instant he stood rooted to the spot, his body going weak beneath the tingling sensation of adrenaline spilling into his system. With a desperate cry, he began to sprint away, impervious to the pain in his leg.

"Help!" he cried, the desperate supplication lost in the deep woods where there was no one to hear.

The bear trailed him in relentless pursuit but did not quicken her pace, or she would have surely captured him at once. Twigs snapped beneath his halting steps, boughs slapped him across the face. Lester lost his walking stick while trying to scramble over a deadfall, but he never released his grip on the pistol, though he knew it would take a miracle—one he was too exhausted to pull off—to drop the huge beast with a well-placed shot. The bear's furry hide was so thick and her body so well-armored with fat that a slug might glance off or enter just far enough to infuriate her.

Lester was a good marksman, but even a shot to the head might be inadequate. He had learned that some bears are like hogs—"double-skulled," the old-timers called it—their cranial bone structure so thick and strong that bullets would lodge in the bone but would not penetrate the brain.

"Help me! God, help me!" he cried, his voice cracking. Stinging sweat trickled to the corners of his eyes and brought tears he was not ashamed to shed.

But Lester's loud cries echoed back to him—mocking him—for he realized that his were the only ears within hearing distance.

A short distance to the north, Min-O-Ta heard a shrill scream coming from the wooded area nestled close to the trail where she had been walking for the better part of the day. She had arisen at first light after a few hours of sleep and was moving at an easy pace. The headdress kept the sun from her face and seemed to capture what breeze there was and bring it toward her cheeks. So she had walked in cool comfort.

Once, she had seen a farmer with his team of horses and a dilapidated wagon. She'd bounded into the woods and hunkered down in a thicket until he passed by, her presence undetected.

Now at the first outcry, she froze, glancing about for a hiding place. At the second, she reacted. Though unable to understand the words, there was no mistaking the message: Someone was in trouble. And Min-O-Ta could not bring herself to turn and run when a human being was calling out for help.

Clutching at the long skirts that had begun to feel comfortable to her as they swished about her feet, she sprinted in the direction of the cries. Several times she skidded to a halt, holding her breath so her own gasps would not obliterate the sound as she tried to get a fix on the location.

When she was due east of the commotion in the woods, she left the trail, wincing as a sharp stick pierced her foot. Even so, she hurried ahead, unmindful of the minor discomfort.

She saw the man almost at once. He was doubled over in pain, grasping at one sapling after another to pull himself along, a pistol gripped in his right hand.

Min-O-Ta's heart faltered. It was that man! The one who had bought her from Jake the day he'd ridden away on his sorrel mare, casting her into an unknown fate.

Her first instinct was to scamper off in the opposite direction. But the man's agonized expression halted her.

"Bear!" he gasped. "Run! There's a she-bear after me!"

Not understanding him, Min-O-Ta stood unmoving and stared. Her eyes widened, but no sounds passed her lips. Then she saw the sow-bear, lumbering through a thicket, headed toward the man.

Min-O-Ta stiffened in shock, but still she made no sound. Peering at the animal, she saw that the bear was rabid! A foamy froth clung to its snout and its jaws worked as if the beast were trying to swallow without success.

"Save yourself, miss!" Lester cried.

Min-O-Ta watched, sizing up the situation. Instead of fleeing, she approached the man as if propelled by an inner force. He screamed wildly, gesturing for her to go back the way she had come.

As she neared the fellow, she realized that he did not recognize her. Satisfied that her primitive disguise was working, relief coursed through her body.

She could see that he was injured and no match for the huge bear. Likely, he had never faced a bear as she had many times, and was unsure what to do.

Min-O-Ta kept silent, aware that the man would not have understood her speech as she did not understand his. Besides, there was no time for talk. She must work fast. Jerking her skirts from the brambles with an impatient yank, she stepped up to him.

He was startled and resisted when she began to pry his fingers from the pistol. But if only because of his weakness and her own determination, she wrested the firearm away from him.

"What do you think you're doin'?" Lester yelled after her as she pressed deeper into the woods toward the bear.

Clenching the pistol in her right hand, its butt comfortingly warm from the man's grip, Min-O-Ta faced the advancing animal. She picked up a stout stob as she circled the bear, who had stopped and was now eyeing her curiously. Studying the beast, she realized that the sow was more confused than angry.

From the years spent in the wilderness with Jake and her mother, trapping and foraging for their living, Min-O-Ta had occasionally encountered various rabid animals. Jake had taught her that there were two natures to the affliction. One form of rabies made the animal furious and irritable, while the other caused lethargy and paralysis.

It was clear to Min-O-Ta that this bear was afflicted with the latter. Her mouth worked, but she seemed weak, incapable of biting. Ordinarily swift, the mother bear was now awkward, moving with a shuffling gait, no match for Min-O-Ta's speed and agility.

Keeping the stob aloft in her left hand, ready to bring it crashing down on the bear's snout, she darted close, lifting the heavy pistol with her right hand, her finger cocking the trigger as she drew a bead on the animal. She knew she had to be exacting with the shot—firing directly into the bear's eye or coming close enough to ram the long barrel into her ear, so that the slug could slam through soft cartilage and lodge in the brain, a comparatively small organ considering the bear's great bulk.

"Are you crazy?" shouted Lester, understanding her intent. "Get away from that animal!"

He pinched his eyes shut, unable to witness the sight of the bear ripping into the foolhardy young woman. But his eyes flew wide open when a loud report roared through the woods, and birds roosting in the boughs abandoned their perches in a flutter of wings.

Lester stared in disbelief as the bear stood, swaying drunkenly, but only for an instant before pitching to the side and slumping forward, coming to a crumpled heap at the girl's feet. Its paws worked spasmodically, as if the supine animal were trying to outrun the pain that had overtaken it.

The girl finally seemed to come to her senses. She skittered away from the outstretched claws and swiftly joined Lester, watching the futile efforts of the bear to rise, only to fall to the forest floor with a thud, making the rasping, gurgling sounds of death.

She gestured toward Lester's hunting knife and he handed it over reluctantly. "What on earth . . . ?" he murmured, staring at the back of her hauntingly familiar smock as she approached the bear.

The blade glinted in Min-O-Ta's right hand. She paused only so long as it took to discern the location of the great beast's heart. Then Lester looked on in horror as she raised her arm and brought the knife slicing downward with what was surprising strength for a woman. The blade penetrated the hide and fatty tissue, and grated as it slid off a rib, then plunged into the pulsing, straining heart.

She leapt back just as a geyser of steamy blood shot into the air, then a few heartbeats later, weakly dribbled to pulse away as the beast's life ebbed away and its suffering ended.

The girl wiped the blade clean on a thick patch of grass. But instead of returning the knife to Lester, with a wordless look in his direction, as if to bid him follow her, she made off in the direction from which she had come.

Lester hobbled along behind her, using for a walking stick the stob she had wielded so threateningly over the bear. The scent of gunpowder from his reholstered pistol plumed around him, acrid in his nostrils but a most welcomed scent.

The girl paused in a marshy area, laid the knife in a shallow pool of water, letting it soak clean. Meanwhile, she located another puddle where she bathed her hands and feet, drying them on fresh clumps of grass before retrieving the knife, wiping it clean, and extending it, handle first, toward Lester.

He shook his head in amazement, wondering if she was an apparition or an angel sent by the Lord. "You're some gal, you know that?"

She looked at him with wide eyes rimmed by dark lashes. Her raven-dark hair created a widow's peak beneath her bonnet, although the bulky head covering concealed what was obviously a thick swath of long hair beneath its folds.

"Who are you?" Lester wanted to know.

The girl stared at him, unspeaking.

Suddenly Lester understood. "Oh, heavens! You can't talk, can you?"

There was no reply.

"Can you hear?" He pointed toward his ear.

The girl nodded.

"Poor thing, then you're a mute, ain't you? Well, I'm right glad for your company, if not your conversation. And I'm beholden to you for my life! The name's Lester . . . Lester Childers." He extended a hand.

The girl stared at it. Then, emulating him, she stuck out her own hand, still damp from the swamp water.

"Come along with me," he invited, "and we'll find your home. Or someone in these parts will know where you belong."

Lester was crippling along the trail, using Min-O-Ta's arm for support, when he spotted a dray up ahead, entering from a side path. Unable to hurry, he waved his arms and yelled loudly. But the teamster, who might be whistling or humming to amuse himself on his drive, did not appear to notice him.

The strange young woman beside him seemed to regard the dray with some apprehension, not responding when Lester gestured in the direction of the conveyance and then pointed to his injured limb to let her know he needed assistance. "Go! Please go!" he begged.

She gave him a long look. Then, without a word, she did as

she was told, though not with the speed and alacrity with which she'd faced the she-bear in the woods.

Lester felt like weeping in pain and frustration when he saw the dray disappearing into the distance. Like as not, there would not be another for a great while.

Suddenly he remembered his pistol. The man was not so far away that he wouldn't be likely to hear the loud report of a shot.

Lester squeezed off a round, then another. He'd just fired for the third time when the dray abruptly halted. The teamster hopped down and looked around, spotted the mute woman, who, in turn, pointed in Lester's direction.

Apparently noticing from Lester's gait that he was injured, the driver turned the team around on the trail and rumbled toward him, motioning for him to climb aboard.

Lester gratefully eased himself into the dray beside the driver.

"You, too, Miss," the teamster invited.

"She's mute," Lester explained.

"She your woman?"

"No, sir. Never laid eyes on her before today. But was right glad to meet up with her. She just saved me from a rabid she-bear!"

"Do tell!" the man gasped.

Lester recounted the dramatic story, sparing no details.

The teamster listened with rapt attention but said nothing more until he'd negotiated the team around again to head in the proper direction. "Arlo Carlson's the name, lad. Welcome aboard!"

"Childers is my name. Lester Childers, though I don't know who the woman is," he said, motioning with his head toward the back of the dray where Min-O-Ta was seated. "But we're both much obliged for the ride."

"Hurt yourself, eh, lad?" the older man inquired, appearing to encourage conversation.

"Sure did." And Lester proceeded to explain his accident.

"Too bad. Workin' for Meloney Brothers, I reckon?"

"That's right."

The man gave a grim jerk of his head toward Lester's game leg. "Don't look like you'll be doin' much of anything for anyone for a while."

Lester gave a tired sigh. "Reckon not."

"Got a wife and young'uns anywhere?"

"No."

"Then you've only got yourself to worry 'bout," the man went on. "So you can be thankful for small blessin's."

With the pain growing worse by the minute, there seemed nary a hint of any recognizable blessings—large or small— Lester thought. "How far ya goin'?"

The man shrugged. "As fur as ya need to go. What about the woman? She's so silent and stoic, a bloke can plumb forget she's around."

Lester nodded, murmured his thanks, and managed a thin smile. What was he going to do about the strange dark-haired woman? "The way my ankle's startin' to throb now that I've taken a load off my feet, I expect I ought to go right to Doc Wellingham's place in Williams."

"Okeydoke. And if the girl ain't from Williams, mayhap some of the townspeople will know where she belongs."

"I'm much obliged, Arlo."

"Takin' you to the good doctor's will give me a chance to meet the sawbones 'fore I have a need for him myself. I hear tell he's a right nice feller . . . and his wife's a purty gal and a boon to the town."

"That she is," Lester said. "I've known Marissa—Mrs. Wellingham—for as long as I can recollect. Her twin sister, too, of course—my boss's wife, the new Mrs. Luke Masterson."

"Do tell!"

Lester satisfied the man's lively curiosity with a recital of the years he had spent in central Illinois, growing up with the Wheeler girls. "And my sister Harmony is Doc Wellingham's nurse. And from what he has to say about her, she's a regular whizbang—plenty smart and purty and country-gal tough." Lester shrugged. "Reckon she gets that from our ma, though she don't *talk* like her. Harmony's had more book-learnin' that anybody in the family."

"Your sister can handle herself if there's trouble, can she?"

Lester chuckled. "Well, iffen she can't think her way out of a strait, I reckon she could scratch or kick her way out!"

Arlo Carlson nodded, then spat into the swaying grass at the roadside and adjusted the brim of his hat over his brow. "Might be a good thing, lad."

Something about the man's tone convinced Lester that there was more to his comment than the words implied, and Lester shot him a puzzled look. "Do tell," he prompted.

"I was in town just yesterday. The latest scuttlebutt has it that there was quite a free-for-all at the Black Diamond the other night."

"I heard the gunfire myself!" Lester said. "But I didn't poke around to find out what it was all about."

"Heard it told that words was exchanged and then one feller, a reg'lar rapscallion, pulled a knife on the other bloke. The man wieldin' the knife didn't know that the other one was packin' iron, and when Billy LeFave offered to slit the gent open from gullet to gizzard, the pistol-packin' feller drew his piece and plugged Billy a time or two."

"So it wasn't just a warnin' shot or a near miss," Lester breathed. "Sorry to hear someone was hurt."

"Maybe the gunslinger only meant to wing Billy, but I have my doubts." The teamster squinted and spat once more. "LeFave's adversary don't usually miss."

"From the sounds of things, it was a clear case of a man defendin' himself."

Arlo nodded and his face twisted into a grimace. "Folks have been mutterin' that the feller should've done the world a heapin' big favor and done away with LeFave, once and fer all! 'Cause he's a killer, pure and simple, and if he lives, he'll be in trouble agin, mark my words."

"Well . . ." Lester wasn't so sure. He knew the value of all life. But he also knew the frustration of seeing good folks die while the evil often seemed to survive and even flourish.

"Well, with you, lad, Doc's got a patient who'll appreciate his services and no doubt be quick to pay for 'em, while Le Fave prob'ly won't bother. And I'd look out for my sister, too, if I was you . . . though I 'spect the doc will see to it."

"LeFave had better wise up about how to treat decent women," Lester warned in a menacing tone, "or he'll have to answer to me, too!"

The man gave Lester a sidelong glance. "Tougher men than you have taken on Billy LeFave . . . and been silenced forever."

The hair on the nape of Lester's neck prickled. "You're not joshin' me now, are you, friend?"

Arlo gave him a look of consternation. "Couldn't be more

serious, lad. Take my word for it . . . that Billy LeFave is a bad 'un. He'd just as soon slit your throat as look at ya."

"Reckon I'll see for myself soon enough," Lester said as cabins and shanties on the very edge of town came into view.

"LeFave's got an eye for the ladies," Arlo continued, warming to his tale. "He'd prob'ly like that 'un ridin' back there." He gave a soft guffaw. "It ain't small talk the man craves from a woman."

Arlo glanced back guiltily, remembering that the woman was mute but not deaf. His startled gasp drew Lester's attention. "She's gone! Now where do you reckon she's run off to?"

Lester shrugged. "Dunno. Maybe she lit out when we came to wherever it is she hails from."

"Yep."

"I would've liked to thank her again," Lester said, feeling strangely bereft, for her sudden departure from the dray seemed to create a new void in his life.

Well, he'd ask around, he promised himself. Maybe Marc or Rose Grant or the owner of the mercantile would know who she was. When he was up and about, he aimed to ride out and properly thank the mute woman and let her family know of her great kindness.

chapter
12

ENGROSSED IN THEIR conversation, the two men in the dray had seemingly forgotten all about Min-O-Ta. When they had neared the outskirts of the small village from which she had fled the night before, she'd silently slid off the back, landing with a rolling step.

With quick movements, she had lain flat in the long grass that rimmed the edge of the dusty trail. When they had rounded a bend, Min O Ta had picked herself up and considered what to do. She was having second thoughts about running away from the kindly flower woman. It would not be as easy as she had imagined to make it alone in the world. She had no tools, no implements, no firearms, and no way to get them. And having seen how helpless a grown man could be in the wild had caused her to realize her own precarious position.

Besides, her stomach was rumbling hungrily, and the berries and edible plants she had swallowed down in the early morning hours had done little to appease her appetite. One thing to be said about the kind woman, Rose: no one left her table hungry!

The large tepee where Min-O-Ta had made beds and helped clean did not belong to her, but within several new dawns, it had almost begun to feel like home, a place where she belonged.

Min-O-Ta sensed that, rather than being irritated with her for her overnight absence, the woman would be happy to see

her . . . especially, Min-O-Ta thought with inherent crafti-
ness, if the woman believed she had merely taken a walk and
become lost!

Of course, there were the garments wadded beneath the
covers. But even so . . .

Too tired to pluck at these knotty problems, Min-O-Ta
chose, instead, to trust that the flower woman would take her
back and continue to keep her safe from Billy LeFave. Min-
O-Ta could continue her friendship with Becky Rose, too,
and the hurt man's yellow-haired sister. Maybe even see *him*
from time to time, in hopes that his view of her would change
and that he would treat her at least as decently as he had when
he'd believed she was the dark-haired woman who had saved
his life! Not that she'd ever tell him of that deceit. . . .

Min-O-Ta's roiling thoughts ceased if only because she was
too exhausted to think anymore. She could consider those
things later, she comforted herself as she hastened through
the dusty streets toward the hotel.

The large tepee looked like a haven to Min-O-Ta as she
moved briskly up the street, climbed the back steps, and let
herself in the door of the cooking room.

The flower woman was stirring a kettle. Seeing Min-O-Ta,
she gasped, the lid clanking into place with her startled move-
ment. "Heavens to Betsy! There you are! Where have you
been? We've been worried sick about you, Joy!"

Min-O-Ta stared, unsure what to say, and uttered one word
in Chippewa, hoping Rose would comprehend. "Lost. . . ."

"Oh, you poor thing!" the woman crooned, enfolding her
in her arms. And in her halting Chippewa, she questioned
Min-O-Ta about the night before.

Min-O-Ta told her story. She had gone for a walk and lost
her way in the darkness. Then, coming upon a man in the

woods, she had saved him from a bear. . . . She chattered on, not realizing that Rose comprehended only about every tenth word and scarcely believed one of them!

"Don't fret, darlin'," Rose dismissed. "You're back now and that's all that matters! Now, there's warm water in the reservoir and you must have a hot bath. You'll feel so much better when you're fresh and clean again."

Min-O-Ta didn't know everything the woman was saying, but she could read the emotions in Rose Grant's eyes, and it warmed her to the depths of her heart. For the first time in her life, she knew what it was to be truly wanted. . . .

"Whoa!" Arlo Carlson called out to his team and hauled on the reins. And with a clank of hardware, the snorting, stomping team of workhorses stopped in the shade of a jack-pine tree in front of the Wellingham residence.

"Here we are, lad," Arlo said, wrapping the reins into place as he stepped down. "Reckon you can make it from here?"

"I'll give it a try."

Even when Lester had shifted his weight on the jarring, jouncy ride to town, he had suffered discomfort. But it was nothing compared to the searing bolt of pain that radiated from his ankle as he tried to move his leg into position to lever himself from the dray. A cold sweat broke out on his forehead and his skin blanched pale beneath his tan.

"That bad, eh?" Arlo asked, studying the younger man.

"Worse," Lester said, gritting his teeth.

"Stay where you are. Better let me hie on in and fetch someone to help. Betwixt the two o' us, we can lug you inside. Doc'll make you more comfortable in no time."

Lester managed to get to his feet, wobbling as he reached out to grip the low cart for balance, and he prepared to hop down. But he hadn't reckoned on landing on a small pebble

that caused his left foot to roll ahead. Instinctively, he stead-
ied himself with his bad foot, and when it made contact with
the ground, he yelped in pain.

"Now you've gone and done it, lad," Arlo sadly admonished.

"Do tell!" Lester snapped.

"For a pleasant-enough appearin' bloke, you're actin'
awful independent, ain't ya? You can accept help from a
spindly mute woman but not from an able-bodied gent?"

Lester flexed his jaw. "I'll thank you for the ride to town
and kindly appreciate it if you'd dispense with the advice!"
Arlo's words had only served to heighten the sense of loss
that Lester felt in the aftermath of losing the dark-haired girl
as he had.

Instead of responding in kind, Arlo merely chuckled.
"You're gettin' a mite cheeky for one in your quandary, lad."
He gave Lester a pat on the shoulder that left him feeling like
an ingrate, although he kept quiet. He didn't know *what* to
say without sounding like an irrational, over-emotional, senti-
mental fool over some woman who, hours before, had been a
total stranger.

"But I ain't holdin' it agin ya, son. Pain'll do that to a
feller. I'll go get some help. . . ."

Ma had raised him with better manners. "Arlo, listen . . .
I'm sorry, real sorry," Lester called after him. "And thanks for
what you've done. I–I don't know what's come over me of
late. . . ."

But deep down Lester Childers knew that was not quite
true. What had come over him was a string of nettlesome
problems and frustrating circumstances, beginning with his
winning bid in Warroad that had made him the biggest loser
of all time.

The last thing he needed right now was to come face-to-face with that half-Indian girl, Joy, who contrary to the name Harmony had given her, had become the bane of Lester's existence! If only she would disappear, and the dark-haired apparition in the woods would return . . .

As he waited for Arlo, Lester steeled himself to face the girl who had cost him his dignity and the price of a really good horse. Even so, he couldn't help wondering what she would look like now. At the thought, he could see the knowing looks of the 'jacks in the dining hall at the lumber camp and hear the flippant remark of the one who'd opined she'd "clean up right nice."

A moment later Arlo and Dr. Wellingham came out of the house, with Marissa in close pursuit. "Oh, Lester, what happened?" Distress was written all over her face. "You're hurt!"

"I think I sprained my ankle. Doc will know for sure. I don't think it's broke . . . but it hurts like blue blazes."

"Sometimes a sprain's worse than a break," Marc added.

With Dr. Wellingham on one side and Arlo on the other, the two men serving as crutches, Lester hopped into the house and down a short hallway, into an examining room, and onto a leather padded table.

"The boot will have to come off," Dr. Wellingham observed at once.

"Cut the boot, Doc, but please spare the leg," Lester joked weakly.

Marc gently eased the leg up and, with a deft touch, he examined the boot that was well broken in but still nearly new. "There's no risk to your leg, Les. And if I cut the stitching at the seam, we should be able to save your boot, too. A good cobbler can repair it good as new."

"Much obliged, Doc. What funds I don't have to spend on new boots can go toward payin' for your services."

Marc smiled. "Don't worry about that, Lester. We can work something out."

Dr. Wellingham touched the tip of a razor-sharp scalpel to the stitching along the side seam of Lester's stout boot. Gently he peeled back the freed leather and, nudging it forward, slid it off Lester's foot. When he dropped it, the boot thudded to the floor.

"I think we can sacrifice a pair of socks to spare you some unnecessary pain," Marc said.

"Cut away," Lester agreed.

With a few quick flashes of the surgeon's shears, the cotton sock was gone, revealing Lester's pale foot in all its puffy, purple glory.

Lester winced at the sight of it. So did Arlo.

"How that must hurt," Marissa murmured.

Marc didn't say a word, but Marissa was watching his face. With his deepening frown, she knew what she had to do. "I'll go relieve Harmony of her duties. You may need her."

"I don't think that will be necessary," Marc said, but Marissa was already out of earshot. "This foot and ankle are too swollen now to do anything," he said to Lester. "We'll get you cleaned up, put you to bed in the infirmary, elevate the leg, and apply cool compresses. And when the swelling goes down a bit, then we can begin wrapping it. It'll be a few days before you'll be able to get up on crutches."

Marc delicately traced his forefinger along the side of Lester's ankle, so swollen that the skin appeared ready to burst. He palpated the ankle, but even though his probing touch was feather-light, Lester flinched and he drew in a sharp breath.

"It appears that the tendon's torn loose, Les. It'll take awhile for that to heal. Bear too much weight on it before it's healed, and there's threat of it tearing loose all over again."

"Tarnation," Lester sighed, this latest defeat just about the last straw.

At that moment, Harmony entered the room. "Lester! What happened?"

"It's a sprain, Harmony," Dr. Wellingham spoke up. "But he'll be all right. Nothing serious and nothing permanent. Just inconvenient."

"Oh, Les, I've been so worried about you being afoot in the woods," Harmony said to her brother. "Thank the Lord it was only a sprain and not something worse. You might have died out there, with no one the wiser. . . ."

"I've heard all this before, Harmony," Lester interrupted, hoping that Arlo Carlson would keep his mouth shut about the bear and the mute woman's daring rescue. "And as you might well remember, I tried to find a solution. But due to a misunderstanding, I have no horse . . . and you have a house-guest." Lester realized that he hadn't seen hide nor hair of Joy since he'd gotten here. Where was she? And it wasn't until he realized that he hadn't seen her that he was aware that deep down he'd wanted to, and he didn't like that unexpected realization at all . . . no more than he did his strange yearning to see the mute woman again.

He decided to bluster on through. "Did she run off?"

"Who?"

"You know who—that white-Indian girl."

"Joy is her proper name. And no, she did not run off. But she no longer lives here."

At Harmony's words, Lester felt a confusing tangle of emotions. Relief, on one hand, that he'd never have to look at the wild-eyed girl again and be reminded of his folly. On the other hand, there was a surprising void as if he'd suddenly been deprived of something before it was even his. "Where is she?"

"She's staying with Rose Grant. From what Becky Rose said, Joy is afraid of a patient who's a resident here."

"LeFave?"

"You've heard of him?" Marc inquired before Harmony had a chance.

"Ain't everybody?" Arlo softly spoke up from the corner. "I hear tell he's a bad 'un. A real bad 'un."

"'As you believe a man to be . . . so shall he be.'" Marc murmured.

"Well, I haven't had a bit of trouble with him yet," Harmony put in.

"He's been unconscious most of the time," Dr. Wellingham explained.

"I don't know if Joy has any real reason to fear him or not," Harmony said. "And I'm not even sure if the story Becky told me is true. But the best she could make out was that when Homer Ames, Rose's intended, had a chance to sit down with Joy, he found out the poor girl fears for her life!"

"Why? What's he to her?" Lester asked abruptly.

"From what Joy told Homer, that wretched Jake put her on the block many times . . . and one of her more recent buyers was none other than Billy LeFave."

"She was *his* woman—a rotter like LeFave?" Arlo gasped in horror.

"No," Harmony said. "Apparently Jake had instructed Joy to sneak away from LeFave and meet up with him somewhere down the trail. And from there, they'd take off . . . with Billy's money."

159

"So I wasn't the only bloke snookered!" Lester exclaimed. Suddenly, oddly enough, he actually felt a bit better. Even felt a bit of a bond with this LeFave, who'd been tricked in the selfsame manner.

"You sure weren't," Harmony said. "Joy is afraid of you, too, Lester. Awed, maybe. She tends to be wary of all men— even Homer—who she seems to like and trust more than most. But she's downright *terrified* of Billy LeFave."

"Why?"

"Because he's put out the word that if he ever came across Joy again, and she refused to go with him, he was going to kill her!"

"He can't do that!" Lester sputtered. "She's as much mine as she is his!"

Dr. Wellingham laughed. "No matter how much money you two fellows spent to acquire the poor girl, Joy belongs to neither of you. And there are enough good men in Williams to defend her rights."

"Joy belongs to no one but herself," Harmony added, "but my hope is that one day she'll give herself to the Lord."

"That *heathen?*" Lester was astonished. "The white Indian with that smelly leather pagan bag around her grimy neck?"

"That 'heathen' will be in church this Sunday, Lester Childers, which is more than can be said for you," Harmony chided softly.

"She's right, Les. You'll miss services on Sunday, for you'll be in the infirmary. Maybe next week . . ."

"But it's too bad you won't be in church on Sunday morning, Les. You might be surprised to see Joy." Harmony's eyes twinkled when she considered the miraculous changes wrought already. "Becky Rose has gotten her to give up that smelly talisman she believed protected her from the likes of

Billy LeFave . . . and you. Mr. Lundsten at the mercantile already has a lovely gold cross necklace on order. We're all donating a few coppers to give it to her as a token of love and faith from the entire community."

Lester swallowed hard. "Count me in, Sis. I'm good for my share."

Harmony seemed surprised at Lester's generosity, considering that it was his investment, which he could ill afford, that had purchased Joy's freedom. "I'm sure that will mean a lot to Joy."

"Why would it?"

"Because Joy thinks you despise her, Lester Childers."

Lester stared at his sister, dumbfounded. "I don't hate her, Harmony, but it's clear as crystal that Joy loathes me. Why, how could I? The girl means nothing to me . . . nothing a'tall, 'cepting she represents four months' lost wages and a candidacy for a position as laughingstock of the town . . . of the entire county. Maybe even the whole blamed state of Minnesota!"

"Why, Lester Childers, if I didn't know better, I'd think you were as smitten with Joy as she is with you."

Lester struggled to sit up on the table, threatening to go in pursuit of his sister, who had darted out of the room. "Harmony, you're joshin' me, ain't ya?" he cried after her.

When she didn't reply, Arlo Carlson, who had observed everything, replied for her, "Your sister's serious, lad, dead serious!"

"OH, HOMER, I feel so *torn*," Rose murmured. "I didn't know a body could feel so happy and so sad all at the same time."

"I know, dear." Homer laid his hand over hers in a reassuring gesture.

"'Course I'm overjoyed that at long last we'll be together. That I'll know the joys of bein' your wife and takin' you as my lawful wedded husband. But for the life of me, I can't figure out how to capture my own happiness without cheatin' all the others I hold dear."

"I understand perfectly, Rosie. It's a trying situation. That's why I've been patient. That's why I've made quick trips to Fargo to attend to business so I could rush back to your side. But a man can't do business like that forever. I need you with me in Fargo."

"But I simply don't know what to *do*, Homer," Rose whispered, her tone heavy with indecision. "So far, I've been wrackin' my poor brain, recitin' the roll of folks in Williams, and I vow, Homer, I can't think of a single soul I'd feel easy about turnin' the hotel over to. Oh, I can think of some who'd jump at the chance to try, but I know I'd never draw a peaceful breath . . . me being so far away and all. . . ."

"Yours aren't easy shoes to fill, Rosie," Homer agreed. "What we need is someone cut from the same bolt of cloth as yourself."

Rose gave a rueful sigh. "Don't I know it? And it may sound vain, but sometimes I think the Lord threw away the mold when he made me. I know I can be a fussbudget, but I'd have to find someone who's partic'lar about keepin' a clean house. . . ."

"By all means," Homer interrupted, "for your patrons have come to rely on the spotless surroundings they enjoy here."

"And I need someone who'd make sure the linens are snowy and fresh. I won't have guests at the Grant Hotel sleepin' on dingy sheets. . . ."

"And that person had also better set a fine table, Rose, for your business is thriving because of the wonderful home-cooked meals you serve at a reasonable price."

"Folks know they can come here for stick-to-the-ribs food," she admitted. "Why, most of the bachelors in this town wouldn't fare near as well if they had to eat their own fixin's!"

Homer chuckled, then sobered. "As a banker, I know you must also find someone as thrifty as yourself to protect profits and secure the business against foolish spending."

With Homer's words of warning, an uneasy silence sprang up between them and Rose shook her head sadly. "It's a tall, tall order, ain't it?" she murmured, her tone doleful even as her eyes glowed with love for the man who sat across from her. At least, she would never again have to face her knotty problems alone.

"The bottom line is, Rose, that there's probably not another woman in all these parts with your talents, the qualities needed to safeguard your business for the future of your children."

"Alas, I'm afraid that's all too true."

"But just because we can't think of anyone doesn't really matter, Rose," he added on a more hopeful note. "The *Lord* knows of our need. We've been praying over the matter, along with all our friends. Surely he'll send just the right person, and we'll know him—or her—when the time comes."

"You're right, Homer, as always." She beamed at him. "I feel better already." Rose checked her timepiece. "Now I'd best scoot into the kitchen and check on the girls. The supper hour is about to begin, and early diners will start streamin' in any time."

"It appears to me that while you had a solid clientele in the past, Rose, with Joy now waiting tables, there are even more folks coming in to enjoy your good cooking." His eyes twinkled.

"Ain't she a marvel, though? I declare, Homer, if you could have seen how defiant and dirty she was when she first got here! Why, it took three of us—Marissa and Harmony and me—just to give her a good drubbin' in the tub the night Lester bought her at that confounded auction in Warroad."

"Well, she has a good deal more than beauty. She's clearly an intelligent young woman," Homer went on. "I'm sure that's why she's picked up at least the rudiments of our language as readily as she has."

"Folks have been nice to her, too, and generous with their gratuities. But then it's only fittin'. She does give good service."

"She and Becky Rose have certainly become close," he observed. "Almost like sisters."

"Haven't they, though? But you helped the girls along by locatin' a copy of the Good Book in Chippewa, as translated by that Indian agent, Henry Schoolcraft. It's laborious, I'll admit, but Becky has been readin' from the English version of the Bible and then manages to sound her way through the Indian version. Joy's learnin' a lot about the Lord, Homer. I have high hopes that she'll accept him as her Savior one day."

"That's my prayer, too."

"And I have reason to believe she may be thinkin' about it," Rose ventured with a sly smile.

"Oh?"

Rose's smile was dazzling. "She threw away that smelly talisman bag you and Becky convinced me I should return to her."

"Praise God!" Homer murmured.

"Joy's become like a daughter to me," Rose admitted. "And I think she feels like we're family and this is her home. I can't bear the thought of turnin' her out into the world. So whoever runs the hotel has to take Joy, too, as an employee who'll more than earn her keep."

"The Lord knows Joy's needs too, Rose," Homer reminded her. "Surely he'll keep it in mind."

Rose excused herself and disappeared into the kitchen.

Homer was savoring a cup of coffee at a corner table in the dining room when Lester came in, his crutches stumping heavily across the floor. "Hello there, Lester!"

"Evenin', Mr. Ames."

Homer made a gesture as if he were waving away a pesky fly. "It's *Homer*, my boy," he corrected. "We're all friends here. Like family. So it's only right and fitting that we be on a first-name basis, wouldn't you agree?"

Lester smiled. "Then Homer it is."

"Care to join me?"

"Don't mind if I do." Lester pulled out a chair.

"Been keeping busy lately, Les?"

"Not as busy as I'd like to be, Homer." Lester tapped his

leg. "I'm up and about now. But I'm still limited in what I can do."

"It'll be awhile before you return to work for Meloney Brothers."

"Yes . . . if I do. To get away from the hospital—and Billy LeFave—I've taken to spendin' time at the livery. I've always loved horses. And Mr. Bonney talked like he could put me to work there when I'm able."

"Glad to hear it, son." Homer leveled the much younger man a long look as if weighing his words. "Rose has been worried about you. And perhaps I shouldn't be talking out of school, but I know she's been thinking you might be avoiding us. And, well . . . we wouldn't want that."

Lester's cheeks reddened. "It hasn't really been that, sir, but circumstances bein' what they are . . . well . . . funds are low, and I let my quarters at the roomin' house go so I could save money by stayin' with Marissa and Marc until I'm well enough to go back to work."

"That's what friends are for."

Lester gave a wry grin. "Well, I'm lookin' forward to going back to work so I won't have to take charity. Marissa and Marc are great folks, of course, and Sis is a treasure, but I can't stomach Billy LeFave!"

"He's getting better, I hear."

"Must be." Lester shrugged. "He's ornery as cat droppin's. I think Marissa's tempted to larrup him with a cast-iron fryin' pan, and even Marc sometimes loses his patience. Harmony seems the only one he can tolerate. But a bloke would have to be a real cad to mistreat a girl as sweet as my little sister." Lester paused. "And it's a good thing. If he didn't treat her right . . . he'd have somethin' more serious than a gunshot wound to worry about!"

"Well, I'm relieved to know it's only finances that have kept you from coming by, Lester, and not personal feelings. But don't let that stand in your way. I know Rose would be glad to extend credit just for the sake of having you back. She's going to miss you when I manage to spirit her off to Fargo with me."

"We're going to miss her, too, Homer. Real bad. Williams won't seem the same without her."

At that moment, Joy appeared and Lester's heart leapt into his throat. He'd seen her a time or two at church and afterward, to do the neighborly thing, he'd spoken like everyone else. At those times, he'd noticed her looking at him, but there had been no mulishness in the green gaze when she'd returned his greeting.

Had he not already seen the evidence of the transformation with his own eyes, he wouldn't have believed it. Her hair, the color of a banked fire, was swept artfully into a coronet of Becky's creation. Her delicate features resembled a porcelain cameo that his ma used to wear. Seeing her now, it was difficult to remember Joy as she had looked that first night—wild and untamed and much in need of a bath.

But there was something else. . . . That calico dress she was wearing looked mighty familiar. Where had he seen it before? Yes! That was it! The woman in the woods had been wearing a garment like this! The woman who had saved him from the she-bear!

Peering more closely, he studied her features. With some kind of blacking applied to her brows and her auburn hair, Joy could be that woman who could not—or would not—speak!

Could they be one and the same? Lester's jaw dropped as the truth dawned.

"Good evening, Les–ter. . . ." Joy murmured in her halting English. "You . . . order?"

"Coffee, black, for now," he replied, watching her closely. "But I'll want something to eat, too." He paused, and a smile played at his lips. "I'm hungry, Miss Joy. Hungry enough to eat a *bear!* A she-bear . . . if you'll be so kind as to *go out and shoot me one!*"

Joy's gasp was all the answer he needed. Her stark, almost fearful stare, locked with his, as he tried to convey wordlessly that he'd keep their secret.

A moment later, recovering from the words that had shaken her to the core, Joy nodded and disappeared, returning a moment later with his coffee.

They were joined almost at once by Rose, her face flushed from the heat and her delight in seeing Lester. "Well, hello there!" she trilled a merry greeting. "What a lovely surprise! My, but we've missed you around here, Lester."

"Hello, Rose. I've missed y'all, too. Marissa's a terrific cook, but sometimes Billy LeFave's carryin'-on wears a bit thin. Plus, I've been pinin' for some of your good home-cooking. I know I'd be in a real quandary if I was forced to decide who was the better cook—you, Rose Grant . . . or my very own ma!"

"*Lizzie Mathews!*" Rose's exclamation was such that both Lester and Homer lurched in alarm and then looked at her as if she'd momentarily taken leave of her senses. "*Lizzie would be perfect!*"

"Do tell," Homer invited, with dawning comprehension, as Lester looked on, wholly perplexed.

"Lizzie's a world-beater of a cook," Rose began ticking off on her fingers. "She's fussy about her laundry. And her husband allowed last winter when they visited in these parts for

Molly and Luke's wedding that I maintained my floors like his wife does, so clean a bloke could eat off 'em if he chose to."

"She does that," Lester agreed, feeling suddenly very homesick for Ma. More lonesome than he'd felt in weeks. But he still wasn't sure what Rose was driving at.

"And she's thrifty, too, as thrifty can be," Rose went on. "She hasn't got much education . . . but then neither do I! But we've got something better—a knack for runnin' a quality operation and watchin' pennies at the same time!" she finished triumphantly.

"That's Ma, all right," Lester rejoined, frowning. What was the woman up to? "She's got a heap of horse sense, even if she didn't have a chance to spend much time in a schoolhouse like some folks."

"Lizzie Mathews is so friendly," Rose pointed out, "that I expect she's never met a stranger. And I've heard her talk about having an itchin' traveling foot."

Lester nodded. "Harmony and I are hopin' to convince Ma and Brad to travel up to these parts again. We figure that with Molly and Marissa both bein' in the family way, they could be talked into makin' the trip again. Ma'll be the nearest thing to a grandma the Wheeler girls' young'uns will have. . . ."

"And Lizzie Mathews has a heart as big as a horse blanket," Rose persisted. "I know she'd love Joy . . . and Joy would adore her. Oh, heavens, Homer, this could work out so well for everyone concerned!"

"It does sound like it, my sweet," he said, gazing fondly at Rose's flushed face.

"Meetin' Lizzie last winter . . . well, it didn't take me long to figure out that gal's a lot like I am. Tries not to see life as one disappointment after another, but a string of steps along a mountain path, leadin' clear up to a fine view from the top!"

Lester nodded slowly, still puzzled. "That's true enough." More than anyone, he knew that his mother had faced the setbacks of life without complaint and with no injury to her robust faith. "Can't help noticin' that you've got Ma on your mind for some reason, and not just to make small talk, I'm thinkin'."

"You're right, Lester," Rose admitted, beaming. "The truth of the matter is, for weeks now I've been siftin' through my mind for one person with all those traits I just mentioned. And in all my acquaintance, I came up with nary a name. 'Til you mentioned your ma's cookin'. And suddenly, I realized she'd be the perfect one."

"Perfect for what?"

"For takin' over the management of the Grant Hotel so's I'd be free to set a date, marry Homer, and move to Fargo! But I couldn't leave 'til I knew the folks I care about would be in good hands."

"Do you think your ma and her husband would consider it, Lester?" Homer wanted to know.

Lester gave an expansive shrug. "You'll have to ask her. But knowin' Ma, if you give her a chance to be near the girls when their young'uns come, stir in the opportunity to ride herd on Harmony and me, add to that the prospect of helpin' a dear friend like yourself, Rose, and heap on the fact that she'll get to feed and shelter a lot of folks and use her talents to run a jimdandy business in your stead . . . well, I have a strong hunch you'll be proposin' an offer she can't refuse."

Homer grinned at Rose. "Maybe the Lord has just answered our prayers. And you, Lester, could live at the hotel with your folks. I'm sure there would be plenty of ways you could help out, even if you end up accepting a position at the livery later on."

"He needn't wait for that!" Rose declared, smacking her fist on the table. "Why, I could use you right now, Lester. I've been needin' someone to do the bookwork and other chores. You'd get your room and board and a bit of money for your pockets, too. What about it?"

"I'll have to think about it. . . ." Lester said. But he was unable to banish the plaguing thought that, if he accepted the offer, freeing him from taking charity and removing him from the vicinity of Billy LeFave, he'd be abandoning his sister, who needed round-the-clock protection. Not only that, but there was the haunting specter of seeing Joy on a regular—a too-regular—basis.

"As soon as the supper hour is over," Rose said with satisfaction, as if the matter were settled, "I'll turn my mind to composin' a telegram to send Lizzie and Brad Mathews, first thing on the morrow!"

"I know Ma'll want to study on it and pray over it for a spell. But she'll give you an answer as quick-like as she's able."

"If it's the miracle we've been praying for," Rose said with confidence, "then make no mistake about it. Your ma's answer will be quick and sure. *Yes!*"

chapter
14

A WEEK EARLIER, when Lester had been at the Grant Hotel visiting with Homer and Rose, his sagging spirits had lifted significantly, thanks to their confidence-inspiring conversation. Knowing that he would be working sooner than he had believed—either helping out at the Bonney Livery or at the hotel—Lester dared to order a meal that now seemed even more delectable due to his surroundings.

Joy waited on him, giving excellent service. So pleasant and efficient was she that, when he had finished and was ready to settle up his tab, he reached deep into his pocket and found a more generous coin than usual to leave as a gratuity.

Lester had hoped that the girl would be pleased when she discovered the silver piece on the table. But he had not expected her to find it so quickly, and he was still in the hotel lobby when she cleared off the table where he and Homer had been seated.

Looking up, he watched her approach, crossing the dining room and entering the lobby with purposeful strides. She appeared vaguely upset—her gaze unswerving, her right hand clenched, her back rigid—as Lester leaned on his crutches near the cash register.

When she reached him, she extended her hand, now soft, clean, and well-manicured, pearly pink nails replacing the broken, ragged stubs that had marked her appearance earlier.

She unfurled her fingers, the silver coin nesting in the palm of her hand. "Here. Yours. Forgot," Joy pulled forth words of explanation in a hesitant cadence.

"No . . . *yours*," he insisted. "I left it there for you."

Joy stared at him, while Lester felt his face grow hot, his overall demeanor proclaiming his discomfort.

Joy's chin was firmly set. "No want. Do enough." And she held the coin under his nose, almost beseeching him to take it back.

But he could not. Would not. "Take it! I didn't mean anything by it. I always leave the serving girl a token of my appreciation."

At the rush of words, Joy looked helplessly to Rose Grant, behind the register, who quickly translated the gist of Lester's sentiments.

Looking faintly hurt, Joy stood poised in indecision, struggling for the polite word. "Welcome."

"Thanks." Lester sighed, wondering how much more confusing things could get.

Rose chuckled. "She'll learn."

Lester watched Joy glide silently to the back of the room. From a shelf she retrieved a cast-off black-and-red baking-powder tin, wrenched off the lid, chucked the silver piece into the container, then replaced it on the shelf.

When it landed with a solid thunk, he detected that the can was almost full. Obviously, Joy had many patrons who appreciated her services, her willingness to learn and adjust, and responded accordingly with more than encouraging words. Apparently she wasn't so reluctant to accept money from others. Could she dislike him so much?

Lester pondered the matter as he made his way to the Wellingham residence, the crutches cutting into his arms, his left leg growing tired as his right leg hung all but useless.

Marissa was in the kitchen and Marc in his study when Lester let himself in. But there was no sign of Harmony.

"Hungry, Les? You missed supper. . . ." Marissa remarked.

"No, thanks. I ate at the hotel, with Homer Ames. He's a good man."

"That he is. Well, since you've already eaten, I'll tend to the dishes. It appears I'm going to have to start cooking slightly larger portions. Billy's appetite has really picked up in the past few days. That's a good sign."

Lester noticed that beneath Marissa's cheerful chatter, she was tense and looked bone-tired. "Like a little help, 'Rissa? I can dry and stack."

Marissa flashed him a smile. "If you don't mind, Lester, thanks. I'd like that."

Lester accepted a linen dish towel as Marissa fetched water from the reservoir in the wood range. "This'll give us a chance to visit a little, too," she said. "How's everyone at the hotel? Seems I don't get over there much anymore. Things are so hectic here right now, or I'm too tired to go calling. Sunday morning services are about the only chance I have to spend a moment or two catching up with friends."

"Rose is fine. Lookin' better than ever. Homer is glad to be back in town after a few days away. But I'm afraid he's an impatient bridegroom."

"Who could blame him?" she asked, plunging a cup and saucer into the hot water.

Lester took the cup and dried it. "Looks like Rose and Homer may end up settin' a wedding date soon . . . if some plans they have pan out, that is."

"Really? How wonderful."

Lester was tempted to share those plans with Marissa but didn't want her to be disappointed if the plans fell through.

"We could use an occasion to get together and celebrate," Marissa continued. "A wedding would be a perfect excuse. Maybe Joy will catch the bouquet! From what Becky Rose says, there are more loggers than ever taking their meals at Rose's place. We all know her cooking has always been a solid draw, but Becky and I think Joy may be the added attraction." She cut her gaze around to study Lester's reaction.

He issued a noncommital grunt.

"And I wouldn't be surprised," Marissa went on, "that once Joy has mastered our language and learned our ways, she agrees to being courted!"

Deep down, Lester knew that it was none of his business. But he also realized—to his dismay—that for some reason the very idea rankled him. And it wasn't that *he* had any designs on the girl. She owed *him* nothing, and he owed *her* nothing. The only history between them was an expensive mistake.

Marissa didn't seem to notice that Lester had grown more silent even as she chattered on with her questions. At her prompting, he managed to provide answers, but his thoughts were far away.

Twenty minutes later, they had finished the dishes and were leaving the kitchen when Marissa asked one last question. "And Joy . . . how *is* she? From what Becky Rose says, she's making noticeable progress."

Lester nodded. "I'd say so."

"Apparently, she's soaking up everything she needs to know like a sponge," Marissa went on. "Why, as stubborn as she was when Harmony came dragging her home, I never expected to live long enough to see such a change."

Lester shrugged. "Harmony's always been real smart about folks, 'Rissa. She tends to see the good and not the bad. It would seem that her instincts when she named the girl might

175

prove true, after all," he conceded reluctantly.

"Her own people named her well, too. In Chippewa, she's known as 'Good Heart,' and from what I've heard, she does have a kind and gentle spirit . . . if a bit feisty at times."

"I'd been told what 'Min-O-Ta' means. And I'll have to admit, the name appears to be fittin'."

As he spoke, Lester was not aware that his voice carried, preceding him, as he and Marissa progressed through the dwelling toward the infirmary. Or that he'd innocently used Joy's Chippewa name by which she'd been known to others.

But that he'd been overheard soon became apparent when there came an angry bellow from a few yards away in the room Lester had once shared with Billy LeFave. "Min-O-Ta! Where is she?! Where is my woman?!"

"Shush, please, Billy," Lester heard Harmony say.

"Shush yourself!" Billy raged at the nurse and then yelled a curse word in front of Harmony that so infuriated Lester his pulse throbbed at his temples.

"That Billy!" Marissa murmured, distraught.

"Min-O-Ta will come back to me . . . or when I find the worthless wench, I'll kill her and she can feed the buzzards!" he shrieked.

"Oh, heavens!" Marissa gasped softly, her eyes widening with fear. "Looks like we've stirred up a hornet's nest. Now he knows we know Joy!"

"I paid good money for that she-dog!" Billy roared.

"Mr. LeFave, I would ask you to kindly temper your speech," Harmony said quietly. "I am paid to provide care for you, but I am not retained to listen to your abusive language."

Marissa rounded the corner, her eyes blazing, and swept into the room like a ship under full sail as Lester bobbed awkwardly in her wake on his crutches. "You shut your mouth, or

176

keep a civil tongue in your head, Mr. LeFave," she hissed, "or I'll brain you with a bedpan! *No one* talks to Harmony Childers like that in *my* presence, do you understand?"

Billy glared at the pretty blonde who had so selflessly bathed him, fed him, and helped care for him. It was clear that a burning anger simmered just beneath the surface, but at the moment he realized that he was at a physical disadvantage and hadn't the strength to carry out his threats. Pitted against an outraged Marissa Wheeler Wellingham, armed with a porcelain bedpan, even tough Billy LeFave would come out second-best. He turned his face away, muttering under his breath.

"You're probably lucky I didn't hear *that*!" Marissa warned. "Now behave yourself, or I'll ask Dr. Wellingham to sedate you so you won't be able to rant and rage. You'll be helpless as a baby . . . more so than you already are, that is."

The mention of his helplessness seemed to unsettle Billy LeFave even more. He turned and glowered at Marissa, his eyes blazing with pure hatred.

"*You!*" he spat the word. "When I'm through slitting Min-O-Ta's deceitful throat, I'll come for you! You'll not be so high and mighty when Billy LeFave is finished with you!"

That was more than Lester could stand. He stumped ahead, intent on protecting his childhood friend in her husband's absence.

Instead, Marissa, with surprising strength, shoved Lester out of the way. Eyes narrowed and flashing warning signals, she drew close to the bed. Although she was a small woman, Marissa Wheeler Wellingham suddenly loomed as large and imposing as Alton Wheeler ever was in the prime of life.

"I'm not afraid of you, Billy LeFave!" Marissa warned. "You think you're so tough? You're a coward . . . do you hear

177

that? A coward! Afraid to stand on your own unless armed with a gun or a knife. Why, in a fair fight, you big bully, I could whip you seven ways for Sunday . . . even while in the motherly condition!"

"Ha! You'd die quickly and whimpering for mercy," Billy said scornfully.

Marissa's laughter was bitter, and Billy could not meet her stern gaze. He flushed dark red as he realized he was being bested by a woman, and there seemed little he could do about it.

"Emboldened by the Lord God Almighty, and protected by him, too, there's nothing you could do to me, Billy LeFave, unless he permitted it. And I don't think he'd grant a bully like you the chance to harm me . . . especially when I'm carrying a young'un who'll be raised up to honor his holy Name!"

"You're crazy, woman!" Billy sneered.

"That's *your* opinion!"

"Aw, you wouldn't be worth the effort it'd take to kill you," Billy said with a gesture of dismissal.

"It's a good thing for you, Billy LeFave, that my husband abides by the Hippocratic oath to the very letter, because if it was left to me, I'd probably throw you out on the street! But my husband operates this infirmary by Christian principles, and he'll do all he can to save your worthless life . . . but not at the cost of his wife and unborn child, or the woman you know as Min-O-Ta!"

With that, Marissa stormed out of the room.

Baffled, Lester glanced at LeFave, who seemed stunned, and then he stumped from the room, too.

"Now you've done it, haven't you?" said Harmony, who had stayed behind. Her words, delivered as a mild rebuke, were without judgment. "You really had no call to talk to

Marissa like that. And like as not, she's already feeling plumb awful for railing at you as she did. That's not like 'Rissa."

"Hmph!" Billy snorted. "All women are like that . . . *she-dogs!*"

"All of them?" Harmony murmured.

There was a long silence before Billy acknowledged the question. "Well . . . except you. You're different."

"Then I'll thank you, William LeFave, to kindly remember that and gauge your speech accordingly. Will you do that?"

Harmony's query hung in the air for some time before Billy LeFave sighed heavily. "I'll . . . try."

Outside, in the hallway outside LeFave's door, Marissa was suffering from a case of guilt. "Lester, let's forget that this unpleasant altercation took place."

"I don't know if I can, Marissa. That was downright ugly!"

"Well, I'm not proud of losing my temper that way . . . but at the moment, I'm still too flaming furious to apologize!"

Lester was appalled. "Wait a minute, 'Rissa! I wasn't faultin' *you*! It was LeFave! After all you and Marc have done for him, he has his nerve, returnin' kindness with contempt!"

Marissa sighed. "I know. But he's a hurting man."

"He's not hurtin' anymore," Lester protested. "At the rate he's improvin', he'll be up and around and a threat to society in a few weeks."

"No matter how his body heals, Lester, Billy LeFave will always have wounds of the soul that only the Lord can heal."

"That's probably true enough. But at the moment, I'd like nothing more than to give LeFave the thrashin' of his life."

"Every time you feel the urge, Les, I'd truly appreciate it if you'd lift up a prayer for him instead. That's what I intend to do from now on. And what Harmony has done from the beginning. She's remembered what the Good Book says: 'A soft answer turneth away wrath.'"

"Well, the man challenges the bounds of decency. . . ."

"Please, Les? I'm going to ask our friends and church family to pray for Billy, too. He's the kind of person who needs our prayers the most. So, Lester . . . promise me you'll pray."

Lester shifted uncomfortably on his crutches and nodded reluctantly.

"Good." Marissa leaned over and impulsively brushed his cheek with her lips. "I knew I could count on you. And one more thing, Les . . . please don't say anything about this to Marc. He's troubled enough about having Billy here as it is. And I don't want to give my husband one more worry."

"Marissa, you don't know what you're askin'. . . but I can see it won't do any good to protest."

"Thanks, Les. I don't want Marc to be tempted to disavow the oath he's taken, out of fear for his own family."

"Then you'd better pray for *me*, Marissa," Lester said earnestly. "And pray that one day I'll have a love of my own . . . and that she'll be as wise and wonderful as you."

There was a sheen of tears in Marissa's blue eyes. "It's a prayer I'll keep on my lips and in my heart. And in return, I ask you to keep an open mind. There's a woman who's exactly right for you. And given time and a trusting heart, you'll find her. . . ."

Lester had almost succeeded in putting the unpleasant scene from his mind by the time he bade Harmony good night and slowly made his way to his cot. At least, now that he no longer required nursing care, he could escape Billy LeFave's presence during the night hours.

"Childers! C'mere!" LeFave hissed through the darkness.

Lester halted in the hallway, torn with indecision. A part of him pitied Billy. A part of him feared LeFave. And a part of him despised the man. "O God . . . give me strength," he murmured.

Then he pivoted on his crutches and entered Billy's room, hesitating in the doorway. "What do you want?" he asked indifferently.

"Your sister, she told me how Min-O-Ta came to these parts. That you bought yourself a woman thinking you were getting Jake's horse."

"So?" Lester inquired, tensing.

"Min-O-Ta . . . I don't like her that well anyway. Wild-eyed. Dirty. Mean-spirited. I paid good money for her . . . but apparently you did, too."

"Alas, I'm afraid you're right."

"I wanta offer you a deal, Childers," said Billy LeFave in a magnanimous tone. "You can have Min-O-Ta, and I'll not dispute your claim. And in return, I get your sister Harmony."

The promise Lester had just made to Marissa left him, and he was filled with a red and raging fury, volcanic in its intensity. "Over my dead body!"

"As you wish, my man! But since you don't like that deal . . . I'll propose another," LeFave called out cheerfully. "I'll have Min-O-Ta . . . and your sister as well!"

His maniacal laughter echoed beneath the rafters of Dr. Wellingham's infirmary where Billy LeFave, whose body was healing, seemed to grow sicker by the day, to the very core of his soul.

chapter
15

"TRAIN COMING! TRAIN coming!" cried Joy, who had been sweeping the front stoop of the Grant Hotel. She bounded into the lobby, her newly acquired decorum all but forgotten in her excitement at raising the alarm after hearing the familiar *whoo-whoo* of the train as it neared a rail crossing east of town.

"The train's coming! The train's almost here!" The hue and cry picked up, swelled in volume, and rolled through the streets.

Shoppers streamed from business establishments. The blacksmith at the livery put down his bellows and untied his apron. The postmaster left off sorting the mail. Farmers tossed down rakes, and housewives left willow baskets brimming with freshly laundered clothes to idle in the sun beneath clotheslines until after the train's departure.

Among those thronging into the street to hurry toward the weatherbeaten platform in front of the Canadian National Railroad depot were those who lived and worked at the Grant Hotel.

"Run tell Molly Masterson the train's a-comin'," Rose ordered her youngest child, Maggie. "The two of you can catch up with us later!"

In the Wellingham house, Marissa, whose ear had also been cocked to hear the mournful wail of the train, put down her knitting and rushed out the door. In her wake was Marc, still trying to adjust his waistcoat and checking the knot in his tie.

"Harmony . . . hurry up!" Marissa cried over her shoulder in the direction of the infirmary. "You don't want to be late today of all days!"

A moment later, her blonde hair swirling about her shoulders, Harmony Childers stepped out of the Wellingham house, hurrying to catch up with her employer and her childhood friend.

Joy, who had been the first to sound the alert, was among the last to depart for the railroad station. She was looking for Lester, who had been working at the hotel for the last three weeks and had been released from the doctor's care just the day before. Now ambulatory, he could manage without crutches most of the time but was instructed to use the devices if the injured ankle gave him trouble.

"Go . . . Les–ter?" Joy asked, spotting him coming into the lobby, shrugging into his best coat.

Seeing the flaming-haired beauty, he smiled and nodded.

She paused and extended her arm, apparently an invitation for Lester to assist her over the rough street. She was becoming more comfortable in white women's shoes after a lifetime spent in moccasins, but she still had her moments of being less than surefooted.

Unspoken between them, however, was the fact that while it would appear to the public that Lester was gallantly assisting the young woman, it was Joy who was actually steadying Lester, allowing him to save face before his friends and to avoid accidentally reinjuring his ankle.

On the way to the station, he reflected on the events of the past few weeks. He had felt some trepidation in admitting to Rose that he couldn't tolerate Billy LeFave for another instant and was wondering if she might be serious about the offer of a job at the hotel. But he had learned that she was not only serious but delighted that he would consider it. And with Marc's and Homer's assistance, he had moved his few possessions into his new quarters.

At first, Lester had been dubious about the idea of being around Joy on a daily basis and figured she felt the selfsame way, but it was soon obvious that they had mutually and silently agreed to a pact of peaceful coexistence.

In the last few days, though, Lester had felt another emotion stirring every time he came into contact with her. The feeling wasn't brand-new, but it was so powerful that his head buzzed when he looked at her. So far, he couldn't give it a name.

Just as Lester had feared, Joy had learned of Billy LeFave's threats. Through the window of the infirmary, opened to admit the cool evening air, Billy's cries had been heard out on the street. News had spread like wildfire, with this the topic of every conversation for days.

It had bothered Lester to see the stark terror etched on Joy's face, and he had wanted to comfort her. But he hadn't known what to say.

Thank God, Homer and Rose had been there to ease her fears. "We won't let him hurt you, Joy," Homer had said. "There are plenty of menfolk in this town . . . and Billy LeFave would have to fight his way through all of us to get to you."

"And more than that, darlin'," Rose said, hugging the girl to her, "you can have the best Protector in the world. Just turn your life over to Jesus Christ and claim him as your Savior and Lord. Then you'll be under *his* protection."

To back up her beliefs, Rose reminded Joy of the stories

they had discussed around the hearth on many an evening. Stories of God bringing his people out of bondage. Miracles worked to save the elect from their evil enemies.

"If he could save Shadrach, Meshech, and Abednego from the fiery furnace, Joy, he can save you from the heat of Billy LeFave's wrath!"

Joy seemed about to be convinced, then the fear returned to her eyes. She regarded Lester, then Rose. "Him! *Here!*"

"Oh, Lester wouldn't hurt you, darlin'," Rose assured her. "Les is a good Christian man."

But Joy shook her head.

Then it dawned on Lester that Joy believed he had come to the hotel out of his own fear of Billy and his threats. He wanted to explain, but his frustration grew as he struggled with their language barrier. Turning to Homer, Lester spoke, while the older man translated in Chippewa. "I'm not really afraid of Billy LeFave. I just don't like him. Can't tolerate bein' around him. That's why I'm here."

Joy thought it over and was about to accept his reasoning. Then the green eyes clouded with confusion once more. "Love one 'nother?" Lester, Rose, and Homer looked at one another in surprise. The girl *had* been absorbing the Sunday sermons!

"It's not easy to love everyone, Joy," Homer said in her language. "Some people are easy to like, and others make it very difficult for us to enjoy them or even put up with them. But the Lord created us all, and it is his will that we love others as the Lord loves us. We need to try, anyway."

Joy turned a solemn gaze on Lester. "Try? You, Les–ter?"

"Well . . ." He felt his face flush. He wasn't sure if he'd tried or not. For an answer he gave a helpless shrug that seemed to say it all.

In the days after that episode, no one brought up the subject of Billy LeFave around Joy. As a result, she was beginning to relax, and Lester was finding himself as much at ease around her as with the Grant family, the Wellinghams, or even his own sister.

He was secretly pleased on the way to church one Sunday, when Joy paused, stayed nearby, and tried in little ways to ease Lester's discomfort and awkwardness in bearing himself about on crutches. It was no wonder she made such a good employee at the hotel, he thought, for growing up as she had—as an Indian and later expected to assist Jake—she had become adept at studying her surroundings, analyzing a need, and attending to it quickly and efficiently.

Lester found that he would have liked to believe that Joy was showering him with little attentions because she was attracted to him . . . as he was beginning to be attracted to her. But the truth was that Joy was as sweet and selfless to everyone else as she was to Lester. And that knowledge, while admirable, did not come without agony, for it was like a double-edged sword. While he wished to mean more to her than other men, he could see that he did not. He was nothing to her.

So he tried to remind himself that she was nothing to him. Only a reformed white-Indian girl whose freedom had been purchased at the price of a really good saddle horse!

The bellow of the train whistle as it came nearer brought Lester back to the present as Joy urged him on. "All right?"

"I'm fine," Lester assured her, feeling a faint throb as he quickened his pace. "I wouldn't miss this for the world!"

Joy's twinkling eyes told him that she wouldn't miss the long-awaited moment either.

He tightened his hand possessively on her arm. She looked

up at him, cocking her head quizzically. He wondered if she believed that it was only because he was tired and in pain, or if she suspected the truth—that he wanted her close to him to enjoy . . . admire . . . protect.

The throb in Lester's ankle was a little more severe when he and Joy arrived on the edge of the knot of people gathered to greet the CNR train as it hove into sight.

"Heavens! Look at all the folks!" cried Rose Grant, who was dressed in her Sunday best, as were many of those present.

"A bell-ringer of a day!" observed a proud Homer Ames.

"Here come Molly and Maggie! Hurry, Molly!" Marissa encouraged her twin, whose limp was more pronounced with the burden of the coming babe.

"Looks like the entire town has turned out!" Marc said.

"Everyone's here except Billy LeFave," Harmony said. "I invited him, but . . ."

"Thank the Lord for small blessings!"

"Who needs him?"

"Like as not, he'd only start another ruckus. . . ."

Further dire predictions were drowned out by the train's noisy arrival. The whistle sounded once more, causing bystanders to cover their ears and move back. Brakes screeched. Steel wheels grated as they grasped at the shiny rails. Cinders, smoke, and steam belched into the air.

A moment later, the train huffed to a halt, and the engineer looked down from his perch in the iron monster and, with a tip of his hat, smiled upon the assembled townspeople below.

"There they are!"

"Ma! Brad!"

"Yoohoo, Lizzie! Good to see you again!"

"Hey, Brad! Welcome back, friend!"

"Glad to have you back in Williams!"

The moment they had all been anticipating ever since Rose Grant had received a telegram from Lizzie, accepting her offer to manage the Grant Hotel, had arrived.

"It's plumb good to be here!" exclaimed a beaming Lizzie, her new straw hat with one rakish feather framed in the door of the coach.

Brad, grinning, stood behind her, waving his fedora.

"Hello, darlin's!" Lizzie cried. "Heavens to Betsy, Brad, I don't know who to grab first!"

Rose jockeyed herself forward and stood beneath the smiling couple. "It seems only fittin', Lizzie, that you start with your own young'uns," she suggested, helping her friend get organized. "And then the Wheeler girls, of course. And barrin' no complaints from the other citizens of our fine town, I'd like to put myself next in line!"

"That's only right, Rose. After all, I'm goin' to be your matron of honor when you marry that handsome man you've loved for so long."

Lizzie, eschewing the little stepstool the conductor had set in place, let out a whoop and leaped from the rail car, to her husband's astonishment. She almost bowled Lester and Harmony over as she pulled them into her arms, exchanging a rash of hugs and kisses.

In her haste, she grabbed up Joy, too. "Nice to see you, honey. I don't recollect you from before, but I'm sure we'll be good friends."

Then Lizzie released the white-Indian girl and reached for the Wheeler twins, who fell on her with affectionate hugs as their menfolk stood patiently by, waiting their turn to greet the newcomers.

"I'm plumb frazzled!" Lizzie said, giggling when she'd hugged and kissed the last of those gathered to welcome them to Williams. "But it's a wonderful and upliftin' frazzlin', that's for sure!"

"The weddin's two days away," Rose said. "You'll have plenty of time to rest up by then. My girl Becky Rose is a real wonder with hair. Iffen you want, she can help you do it up for the big day."

"You'll be a beautiful bride, Rose. And I'm honored to be your matron of honor. Makes me think—I've always been the bride but never a bridesmaid! I had a real bona fide honeymoon with Brad. And now, thanks to you, I get a chance to be part of a weddin' party!"

"Liz is wondering what other mountains she can climb before the Lord calls her home someday," Brad mused.

"He's right as rain. My mama always used to say, 'Children, when opportunity knocks, have the common sense to answer the door!' I've lived that way all my life and, when I got your telegram, Rose, I saw it as opportunity come callin'."

"The town's going to be sorely grieved to lose Rose," said Luke Masterson. "But the loss will be a little easier to take since we're gaining a Lizzie."

A ripple of light laughter from the crowd that had turned out to welcome them warmed Lizzie's heart, and she knew that, no longer than she'd known most of these folks, she had already won a place in their hearts. "Oh, Brad, I just know we're goin' to be happy here! And you, Homer," she warned. "We're goin' to hold you to your word. You'd better bring Rose back to these parts when you retire from the bankin' world."

"Lord willing, Lizzie," he called out, "it's only a matter of time."

"Now, neighbors, you're all welcome to stop by the hotel for a few refreshments and some more catchin' up with the

Mathewses," Rose issued a blanket invitation. "Today's a day for celebratin'!"

Eventually the guests drifted back to their tasks and allowed the weary travelers time to get reacquainted with their family and closest friends.

Joy had stuck close to Lester all afternoon, seemingly enjoying the hubbub, yet keeping her distance.

"Lester Childers!" Lizzie addressed her son with mock gravity. "What've you been hidin' from us? A gorgeous gal on your arm, and you've said nary a word to your ma and pa about her? Won't you introduce us to your gal?"

"She's not my gal. Well, I mean, not *really*, Ma. I may have accidentally bought her, but . . ." His face flaming, Lester realized that the more he tried to explain Joy away, the worse the story sounded.

Lizzie stared at him, incredulous. "You *bought* a woman, Lester? *Bought her?!*"

"Ma, it ain't like it sounds. . . ."

"Well, I should hope not, Lester Childers. Your explanations had better be good, 'cause you don't only have me to account to, but the Lord, too!"

"Well, Ma, see . . . sometime back, I took Harmony to Warroad, and all the way, she was pesterin' me to buy a horse. . . . "

Lizzie's expressive face registered her changing state like a kaleidoscope of emotion as she listened to the preposterous story and found herself believing it.

She whooped with laughter when he ended his tale. "You mean you bought a girl instead of a horse?" she asked and gave Joy an assessing glance. "Well, Son, I've always known you were a good judge of horseflesh. But it appears you've got an eye for quality womanhood, too."

"Ma, it was an accident. Joy's nice, but I ain't holdin' her to the deal. It was an honest mistake."

"If it was an honest mistake, Lester Childers, then don't go makin' another one."

Lester frowned in confusion.

Lizzie glanced from her son to Joy and back again. "If you can't see it, then I ain't a-goin' to bother tellin' you, Lester Childers, for fear of being tempted to do it with a two-by-four the way Jeremiah knocked sense into a stubborn mule. Wise up, Les. After all, your ma's taken some pride in the fact that over the years she ain't raised up any fools!"

After giving Lester and Joy a quick hug, Lizzie swept from the room. Without looking back, she looped her arm through Brad's as he waited for her at the base of the stairs leading to their rooms on the second floor.

"What's she talkin' about?" Lester asked Rose and Homer with an imploring look.

"The fact that, for an ex-timberman, you now seem unable to see the forest for the trees," Homer said, his voice cryptic, his eyes amused. Frustrated, Lester turned to Joy, who had been lost during the lively conversation. "Do *you* know what she's talking about?"

She paused only a moment. "Trees?" she helpfully supplied her newest word.

chapter 16

"WHO IS IT?" Lizzie sang out in answer to the knock at the door of her suite in the Grant Hotel where she and Brad would be living now. She was putting away the clothes they had brought, using these few moments while Brad was off with Homer to look over their new town.

"It's me, Mama. Harmony!"

Lizzie flung the door wide and hugged her only daughter. "My, how you've grown up, Harmony, honey! Your papa would be so proud of you. Not that he doesn't already know how well you're doin'. It's my belief that he's been lookin' down from heaven, while your mama had to travel to these parts to see for herself. Why, I hear tell you're the pride and joy of this town, and apparently, you're Doc Wellin'ham's right hand, too!" Lizzie said, beaming with pride.

"I do my best," Harmony replied, her tone modest.

"Well, you've got healin' in your heart and spirit. Granny Fanchon had it. And I have it. But you've got it by the pecksack full."

"Times have really changed, Mama. Many of yours and Granny's methods work just fine. But there are so many other things we can do now—what Dr. Marc calls 'the advance of modern medicine.'"

Lizzie hung a blue calico frock in the armoire and turned to look at Harmony. "I'm lookin' forward to gettin' an eyeful of those miracle contraptions. A time or two, when we had to visit the sawbones in Illinois, I wanted to ask about the new-fangled gadgets settin' around in his office. But I figgered he was a busy man and would think me plumb pestery."

"Well, we wouldn't think so, Mama. I'd love nothing better than to show you around the infirmary. Just let me know when."

Lizzie consulted the brooch timepiece pinned to her dress. "We'd best have a look-see right now, 'cause tomorrow Rose and I will be siftin' flour and strewin' confectionary frostin' from one end o' the kitchen to the other, gettin' ready for the weddin' feast."

"Come on then, Mama. Let's get started."

Lizzie placed a stack of petticoats in a drawer and turned to follow her daughter into the hallway. "On the way, Harmony Childers, would you mind explainin' your version of how Lester managed to up and buy hisself a woman?!"

"He admitted that to you?"

"Yessirree, he did!"

"I'm surprised."

"So was I. But maybe he figgered he'd better, since his sister had prob'ly already beaten him to it."

Harmony sighed. "Actually, it sort of slipped my mind when I was writing, Mama. We've been terribly busy at the infirmary of late. Several women have given birth. We had a logger with a cut hand that required stitches and then Lester's sprained ankle."

"Ain't got any patients at the moment?"

"Well, we sent a new mother home yesterday morning before the train arrived. And we do have a patient who's been with us for a while now. . . ."

At the tone in her daughter's voice, Lizzie shot her a questioning glance. "What is it I should know about this patient that you ain't tellin' me, child?"

The words poured out in a torrent. "Oh, Mama, he drives Marissa to distraction. Marc loses patience with him, too. And sometimes I get so nettled with him that I wonder why I even bother. And Ma, if he sasses you as he does real often, *you* may even be tempted to grab him up, haul him out behind the woodshed, and give him the thrashing of his life!"

"That bad?"

"Worse!"

"Hates everyone, does he?" Lizzie asked in an arch tone.

"*Everyone*," Harmony admitted. "Just seems to hate me a little less than most others. . . ."

Lizzie nodded sagely. "I've seen that sickness in folks afore, and there ain't a physician alive that can cure it . . . exceptin' the Great Physician himself." She shook her head. "It'll take a miracle . . . one only he can bring about."

Marissa met them when they reached the door of the infirmary, and Marc quickly left his study to greet them. "Since Harmony knows the infirmary better than anyone, Miss Lizzie, I'll leave you to her expert guidance," he said and excused himself.

A bored Billy LeFave darkly watched from his hospital bed as Harmony showed her mother through the examining rooms, the operating area, and the delivery room, passing by the cubicle where he was confined.

"This your patient, darlin'?" Lizzie asked, when it seemed that Harmony was about to leave without introducing her to the sole occupant.

"Yes, Mama. This is Billy LeFave. Billy . . . my mother, Lizzie Mathews."

"How d'ya do, Billy?" Lizzie said enthusiastically, and put out her hand.

Billy looked at her as if he couldn't decide whether to spit in her open palm or accept a friendly grip. Finally, he did the latter.

"What happened to *you?*" she asked.

Silence. "Gunshot wound."

Lizzie winced. "That must've hurt like blue blazes. But from the looks of you, you'll be up and around in no time."

"Not a moment too soon," Billy grunted. "I hate this place. I hate this town. I hate—"

"Oh, you've got the order o' things all wrong!" Lizzie interrupted, seating herself on the edge of Billy's bed while Harmony hovered in the background. "First and foremost, son, it's clear to me you hate *yourself* with a plumb passion. After that, I reckon you hate the way you've lived your life. And after that, you prob'ly despise the people you've met along the way. . . ."

Billy stared at Lizzie, the dark wings of his brows lowered over sultry eyes. There was no life in the sullen gaze, only a smoldering anger that threatened to erupt at any moment.

Lizzie pressed on. "You don't hate the good people of this town, Billy LeFave. What you *really* hate is the way you act that puts fear in 'em. And knowin' they fear and resent you, you hate 'em all the more. It's what my mama used to call a deadly circle. And, Billy, a circle never ends!"

His expression barely changed, but she could tell he was listening.

"The only reason you hate so much is 'cause no one's ever taught ya how to love. But at your age, young man, I'd say it's high time you learned." Lizzie studied the chiseled features, the strong jaw and thought she could discern that he was softening a little. "I know my daughter Harmony's been trying to help. . . ."

He nodded. "She's been good to me," he admitted, "when no one else would put up with me."

"Oh, yes, they would, iffen you'd let 'em. But I 'spect you was too busy keepin' up your monster image. Big galoot that you are, you ain't figgered out yet how to let someone love ya . . . and it looks like you sure ain't a-goin' to risk lookin' like a fool in the process."

Silence stretched between them almost to the snapping point.

"Nobody's ever . . . loved me," Billy began, his voice cracking, his lower lip trembling with scarcely pent-up tears.

Lizzie looked into the stricken face. "Surely your mama did, son."

"I never knew my ma," Billy went on. "She and my pa, the best I can piece it together, were killed by Indians when their wagon was set upon as they moved west. I was too little to remember them, too small to take care of myself, and a couple of old trappers took me along with them."

"Then surely *they* come to love you . . . tadpole that you was. . . ."

Billy's eyes flashed fire. "*Love* me?" he scoffed. "They had to have hated me to do the things they did! The years I was with them, I did the scut work around camp—hauled heavy loads, even did the washin' and the cookin' when I was older—and when they were drunk . . . well, they used me in ways no man should use another. . . ." He broke off, his expression veiled. "I hate them. *I hate them!* And I hate myself most of all . . . for lettin' it happen!" And with that, Billy LeFave broke down and began to weep.

Lizzie leaned over and folded him into her arms, pillowing

his dark head against her breast as he sobbed out the grief of twenty years. Grief that had never resulted in the shedding of tears but in a hidden rage that had been like a cancer eating away at his soul.

"It wasn't your fault, Billy-boy," Lizzie crooned. "You was just an innocent and trustin' little boy! The sin was theirs, Billy, not yours. But the Lord kept you goin'. He give you the strength and will to survive, because he wanted you to know that even if you was left without any livin' kin a'tall, it didn't matter. You could always be his beloved adopted son iffen only you'd take him as your lovin' and forgivin' Father."

Billy wiped his eyes with the back of his hand. "But I feel so awful, Lizzie . . . so dirty . . . so ashamed . . . not just because of what they did to me . . . but what I've done, too—hurtin' others so they'd know what it was like."

"Of course you do, Billy. That's what bein' sorry for your sins feels like. But it's good to hurt as bad as that makes you hurt, for then a body is willin' to turn to the only one who can help him change—Jesus. Deep down, William LeFave, I know you're a man who's seekin' the Lord. And as bad as you want *him*, Billy, he wants *you* much, much more."

As Lizzie held Billy close, she explained the rudiments of faith, quoting Scriptures that were familiar to him only because he'd heard Marissa read them by the hour. How many times had she droned on and on, patiently reading the Good Book, while he'd surprised himself by refraining from shouting at her to shut up!

"It's like this, Billy," Lizzie said softly, straightening as he put his head back on the pillow. "That bullet wound of yours . . . well, Doc Wellin'ham done the best he could, but there'll always be a scar. When it comes to folks healin' other folks, it's like a nail hole. You can fill it with putty, stain it, and lac-

JOY IN THE MORNING

quer it. But if you look close—no matter how good a job's been done—you can still see that little hole. Now God don't just patch up a feller. When he does the healin'—body or soul—there ain't no scars a'tall!"

Billy heaved a deep sigh. "Maybe that works for other folks, but not for me. I've done too much . . . hurt too many people. . . . I don't deserve—"

"Now you listen to me, Billy LeFave! Orphaned as you was at a tender age, the fact is you've always had a Father's love. He's been there all the time. You was just too blind—or mul-ish—to see!"

He groaned. "But I've missed having a pa. Missed having a ma. Maybe if I'd had a ma, I'd be more like Lester and Harmony. Decent . . . instead of a desperado."

"'Course you would, darlin'," Lizzie said. "Desperate peo-ple do desperate things. 'Twarn't all your fault—the straits you was put in and the choices you was forced to make. But you're plumb right about havin' a mama. Why, if you'd been mine, I'd have raised you up to know and love the Lord. . . ."

Lizzie paused as an idea formed. "Why, Billy LeFave, why didn't I think of it afore now? *I* could be your ma iffen you'd have me. My lands, 'twouldn't be the first time! Me 'n' my first husband, Harmon Childers, adopted a baby boy when his folks was killed in a cabin fire. That boy, Maylon, is dead now, too. And I can tell ya that he may not have growed 'neath my heart like Lester, Harmony, 'n' their little brother Thad, but he sure as shootin' growed *in* my heart! And I loved him like my own. Love's like that. The more of it ya give away, the more ya have to give."

"You mean it?" Billy murmured, his moist eyes riveted on hers.

With a rip-roaring laugh, Lizzie gave Billy LeFave a bear

hug. "You bet your bedpan I do, son!" she said. "'N' one thing you need to know about your ol' ma—Lizzie Mathews speaks the unvarnished truth. 'N' she's been known to back it up with the touch of a willow switch or a hug 'n' a kiss, whichever one's needed at the moment."

Billy couldn't help laughing.

"But I'll tell you a secret, Billy," she confided. "I can prob'ly count on the fingers of one hand the number of times I've had to apply a willow switch to drive a lesson home, while I'd have to be an educated woman to count the hugs and kisses I've given away!"

"I can see why the whole town's crazy about you," Billy murmured.

She smiled, her eyes crinkling at the corners. "It's nice to be loved, ain't it?"

Billy thought it over, beginning to believe Lizzie meant everything she had told him. Just as he now believed that he was accepted by her daughter, too. "Yeah . . . real nice," he said, his tone husky. Was that the way the Lord worked, too, loving folks even when they were not fit to be loved?

"Now, I don't want to overstay my welcome. I'd best clear out o' here," Lizzie said in a matter-of-fact tone, peering at him through squinted eyes. "But it's my guess you'll be well enough to be up in time for Homer and Rose's weddin' and reception the day after tomorrow. And I 'spect Doc Wellin'ham may even grant permission for you to 'company Harmony and the others to church on Sunday."

Suddenly Billy's optimism seemed to vanish and despair set in. "I'm not sure I can do that. . . . I know how this town feels about me. Most are sorry that bullet didn't finish me off."

"And out of your own mouth and by your own actions, you've begged 'em to feel that way. They're fair folks, Billy.

They'll forgive the past and be generous with the future iffen they know you're tryin'. Can I count on you to be in church on Sunday mornin'?"

"What if the townspeople don't want me there?"

"They'll want you."

"But what if somebody says something spiteful?"

Lizzie laughed. "Billy LeFave, one thing I discovered when I arrived on the train today is that in this little town, Lizzie Mathews is held in high regard. With me on one side o' you and my dear husband Brad on the other, they wouldn't dare! Now, then, you'll be there?"

He sighed. "I'll be there."

"I'm holdin' you to it," she warned. "And we'll consider your presence in the church at Rose and Homer's weddin' the day after tomorrow a practice session for the big day!"

"I don't have anything decent to wear," Billy launched a logical protest.

Lizzie made a piffling gesture and eyed him up and down with the skilled scrutiny of a seamstress well aware of her abilities. "Don't you trouble yourself over such a triflin' matter, Bill," she said. "Why, 'twixt the wardrobes of Brad, Lester, Marc, and Luke, I reckon we can get you decked out like a regular Lil' Lord Fauntleroy! What this town's done on Joy's behalf, they're willin' to do for you, too."

"Joy . . ." Billy flinched at the sound of her name. "Would you tell . . . Min-O-Ta . . . that I want to see her . . . uh . . . *need* to see her?"

"Sure," Lizzie agreed. "I'll tell her just as soon as I hie myself on back to the hotel. And I'll spell her in the kitchen so's she won't have no excuse not to come."

"Thanks," Billy said, the word foreign to his tongue, but one that tasted very, very good. "Thanks . . . Ma."

Lizzie blew him a kiss on her way out the door.

Thirty minutes later Joy, relieved of her duties by a strangely silent Lizzie, walked over to the Wellingham residence on Lester's arm. Brad, who was eager to learn the hotel routine as soon as possible, was more than happy to fill in for him for an hour or two.

"Come in, Min-O-Ta," Billy said, slipping easily into the Chippewa language the moment he saw her.

Joy did as she was told, leaving Lester to idle away the time with Marissa in the kitchen.

"Close the door."

Again, Joy obeyed, though a gleam of reluctance showed in her eyes. In her native tongue, she spoke with a quiet confidence that Billy had never seen in her before. "I am not afraid of you," she warned. "I used to fear you, but now I know that you are a mere mortal, no match for the one who protects me now—the Great Spirit who sent his Son and the Holy Spirit to me. They have a claim on me. You do not. And Lester does not!"

In a quick flurry of words, Joy assured Billy that she'd carefully saved her wages and gratuities. "I have almost enough to repay Lester what he lost to Jake when he received me instead of the horse he coveted. And when I have repaid Lester, then before my God, I vow that I will also repay you, Billy LeFave."

Joy was not prepared for Billy's next words. "Any debt that you might believe you hold toward me is forgiven, Min-O-Ta. Nor do I wish to harm you. Repay Lester if you wish, for his was money earned by honest labor. The money I lost to Jake was taken from others as craftily as he weaseled it from me. You owe me nothing."

Joy was wary. "Do you speak the truth?" She had been

tricked so many times before and had long known Billy's reputation for ruthlessness. Could it be true? Or was it just another ruse?

"It is true," he insisted. "Lizzie Mathews is a wise woman. She says I cannot expect to be forgiven until I am willing to forgive. If Harmony's mama is right . . . and this Lord you speak of can love and accept me . . . then perhaps others will, too."

"They have accepted me," Joy said quietly. "They can accept you, too."

An old expression of mistrust and defiance flickered briefly across his face.

"But you must change," she warned.

He spread his hands helplessly. "I don't know how."

"They," Joy said, gesturing, as if to take in the entire town beyond these four walls, "will help you. Watch them. Do as they do. Act as they act. They are good people, Christian people. It will make you happy to become one of them."

Billy regarded Joy, his once-steely gaze softened with the moisture of welling tears. "That's what Lizzie says. Harmony too."

Hesitantly he reached out and, with his forefinger, gently touched the golden necklace she was wearing. It had not left her neck since the townspeople had presented it to her a week ago at the end of a church service, when Joy had gone forward to commit her life to Christ. "Pretty," he said.

She drew back involuntarily, fearing that he might take it from her. "It means much to me," Joy replied. "They say it is a symbol of Christ's love when he died for me on the cross. And it is a reminder of my many friends in Williams who loved me enough to give me this gift."

"Would it spoil the gift to know that I'm one of those friends?" Billy asked gently.

Joy drew in a breath and her eyes widened in surprise. "No. . . ." It was almost too much to take in. Her fingers caressed the pendant hanging from the golden chain. "Knowing that gives it greater value."

Quickly, before she could lose her courage, she leaned forward and brushed a soft kiss of peace on his cheek. "God be with you, Billy LeFave."

"And with you, Min-O-Ta."

Joy was almost to the doorway when Billy spoke, causing her to halt and spin around in her tracks. "He . . . loves you, Min-O-Ta."

"Yes, I know the Lord loves me, Billy. And he loves you, too."

"No, I mean there's a *man* who loves you, Min-O-Ta. A man made of flesh and blood."

Joy stared at him, perplexed.

"Lester Childers," he went on when it appeared she did not understand.

"Oh, no. You are mistaken. He purchased me. But he does not love me."

"He can't see it, Min-O-Ta. Nor can you. But Harmony has seen it. And Lizzie knows, too."

Joy stared at Billy, regarding him with her penetrating gaze. Was this some kind of trick? Was he trying to ensnare her with the desire of her heart, knowing it would be the bait she would not be able to refuse?

But such doubts were part of the past, part of the old Min-O-Ta. She was different now. She was new. She was Joy. She must be vigilant to resist the old thoughts and ways so as to learn more about this fresh new life in the Lord.

203

Billy would have to do the same. And she would do what she could to help him. It would start with believing that what he had said was true. "Thank you, Billy, for what you have told me today. I am no longer afraid of you. You are my friend."

He smiled in relief. "And you are mine."

"Rest now. You are tired," Joy observed.

Billy sank back against the pillow. "Yes, I must rest so that Dr. Wellingham will let me attend the wedding day after tomorrow. . . ."

"And services on the Lord's day," she reminded him.

chapter

17

"WHAT A GLORIOUS day for a weddin'!" Lizzie cried as she left the little log church and stepped out into dazzling sunshine. "And what a grand ceremony it was!"

The newlyweds—Mr. and Mrs. Homer Ames—were surrounded by a crush of family and friends vying for a chance to offer hugs, kisses, and congratulatory greetings.

"I do declare, this is about the happiest moment of my entire life!" Rose announced.

"My happiest is yet to come," Homer said, taking his svelte bride's hand, now adorned with a golden wedding band placed there during the nuptials conducted by the Reverend Edgerton. "For I'll still be counting myself the luckiest man in the state of Minnesota when we're celebrating our fiftieth anniversary!"

"The joy is only beginnin'," Rose said. "We expect to see you all at the hotel for a jimdandy reception before Homer and I leave on the eastbound train for our honeymoon in Winnipeg."

"Do come," seconded Lizzie. "We've got fruit punch, coffee, tea, and a king's assortment of tasties to tempt even the fussiest appetites!"

"Let's go!" chorused a bevy of youngsters, who were familiar with Rose's cooking.

Leading the way in their decorated carriage were the Ameses, Rose clinging to Homer's arm with one hand and her bouquet of flowers from Molly Masterson's rose garden with the other, while the citizens of Williams progressed toward the Grant Hotel, which was festooned with colorful streamers for the occasion.

When they arrived, Lizzie took over with brisk efficiency. "Now you just enjoy your guests, Rose," she ordered the new bride, "and don't you worry about a thing. I can handle it. Why, I feel as much at home in your place as I felt in my own house."

Homer chuckled. "That's good because it's going to be your home for quite a spell."

"What an adventure!" crowed Lizzie. "It's plumb excitin', ain't it Brad? It's like startin' over ourselves when I thought we was too old to be of any use. Heavens to Betsy, who'd have ever thought it? Me—Lizzie Mathews, wife and mother —bein' a bona fide business person!"

"We'll rest easier every day, just knowin' you and Brad are in charge here," Rose said with a happy sigh.

"Know what you mean, Rosie," Lizzie said. "It made my own answer a heap easier to come by when Brad 'n' I talked to Lem Gartner, an elderly bachelor man in the neighborhood, and he allowed as how he'd be tickled to move in with Thad and the young misses. Lem can watch after 'em and be there in their pa's stead. And our young'uns can look after Lem Gartner, too, bein' as I won't be there to keep an eye on him myself. He's getting on up in years, though I reckon he'll have a lot of good 'uns left, Lord willin'."

"We're going to miss the folks back home," Brad said.

"Ain't like we won't see 'em ever again," Lizzie comforted him. "'Sides, looks like we might be needed here in more ways than one!"

Her eyes and Brad's were drawn to the corner of the room where Lester stood with Joy, an amused grin on his face, adoring highlights in the green gaze she gave back to him. She was struggling once more to master the new words Lester was patiently trying to teach her.

"Could be," Brad mused, and gave a nod toward the punch table, where Harmony was serving, her attention riveted on Billy LeFave. LeFave was all slickered up in a store-bought suit on loan from Marc for the occasion. Handsome as he was, he was visibly ill at ease in the midst of the merrymaking, intent on watching his manners and his mouth, lest he make a social blunder and jeopardize the sudden acceptance he was being accorded.

"We're goin' to be real happy here," Lizzie said for the umpteenth time as she tucked her hand in Brad's and dreamily laid her head on his shoulder.

At that moment, Rose and Homer, who had slipped away to change into their traveling costumes, reappeared with their valises. "Time to catch the train!" she announced.

"You're all invited to see us off," Homer said, "and then return to the hotel for more food and fellowship. The party isn't over!"

"We wouldn't miss seeing you off for the world!" their friends assured them.

Outside, Homer struggled with the valises as Rose juggled her bouquet of roses.

"You've got to throw your bouquet, Rose! It's a tradition!" someone called out.

"Then gather down below, you single girls!" Rose trilled.

A number of young women, giggling and jostling, moved into place on the sidewalk below the front stoop.

Rose closed her eyes. "One . . . two . . . three . . ." Her right arm arched up and the roses sailed into the air, releasing a flurry of petals.

Harmony Childers caught the bouquet, but only in the act of preventing it from colliding with her face.

"Harmony caught the bouquet! Harmony's next!"

"Oh, no, I'm not!" she declared firmly. "You all know I'm married to my work. I want to be a nurse . . . not a wife!"

In the face of their razzing and fun-filled joshing, Harmony, as if she had need to rid herself of the challenging bouquet, thrust it at Joy, forcing the flowers into the white-Indian girl's hands. "I may have caught it, but I'm giving the bouquet to Joy!"

"Does that count?" someone inquired.

"Who cares?" Rose spoke up, breaking the tension. "It's just a silly ol' superstition! C'mon! The train's comin'!"

Joy nestled her nose in the fragrant flowers snipped from bush starts that Molly had brought with her to Minnesota and shyly looked up from the satiny blooms at Lester.

"You . . . walk?" she questioned, nodding toward the depot some distance away.

Lester took a first awkward step forward. His leg was still tender, but it was getting stronger every day. So was his love and admiration for the good-hearted woman by his side. When had it come to him that she was the fulfillment of all his dearest dreams and prayers? "Joy . . ." He spoke her name softly, a name that suited her.

He'd grown accustomed to seeing her face at every meal-time at the Grant Hotel.

Joy at noon.

Joy in the evening.

And as Lester Childers' gaze swept heavenward, he gave thanks from the depths of his heart that if the Lord smiled on him, it would soon be his right and privilege to awaken each dawn to . . . Joy in the morning.